I0602081

*A mystery thriller with twist and turns
that will have your heart racing*

The Chronicles of
Integrated Friends

Just when you think you know someone

A Novel

Author Rosej

An Imprint of Ozion Publishing Group LLC

This book is a work of fiction. References to real people, events, establishments, organizations, or locales are intended only to provide a sense of authenticity and are used fictitiously. All other characters, and all incidents and dialogue are drawn from the authors imagination and are not to be construed as real.

THE CHRONICLES OF INTEGRATED FRIENDS. Copyright © 2020 by Author Rosej. All rights reserved. No part of this book may be used or reproduced in any manner whatsoever without written permission except in the case of brief quotations embodied in articles and reviews.

Ozion books may be purchased for educational, business or sales promotional use. For information, please email us at info@ozionpublishing.com

ISBN: 978-17364732-0-7 (Hardcover)
ISBN: 978-17364732-1-4 (Paperback
ISBN: 978-17364732-2-1 (Digital)

Library of Congress Control Number: 2020925901

FIRST EDITION

Book Cover Design by SymoneRae Designs

Printed in the United States of America

Published by Ozion Publishing Group LLC
921 E. Dupont Road, Suite 793
Fort Wayne, Indiana 46825

Visit my website at www.authorrosej.com

For Rochelle Chapman Holliness (Rocky)

A friend is a close companion on rainy days,
someone to share with through every phase....
Forgiving and helping to bring out the best,
believing the good and forgetting the rest.
A friend is a gift whose worth cannot
be measured except by the heart

Author unknown

RIH my friend

CHAPTER ONE

Intro

VICTORIA ELLIS

Intro

Thirty-one years old, five foot, six inches, has a lean build, yet curvy in all the right places. She came to Chicago from San Mateo, California as a finance major. She has an undergraduate degree from North Western University in Finance and continued to complete an MBA. She started her career in banking back in high school and worked part time at Waterfront National Bank during college. She is now the president of Waterfront National Bank of West Loop.

She is from a wealthy family, both parents have successful careers. Her father owns his own investment firm; her mother is a high-end real estate broker, so the financial language is what she grew up hearing around the dinner table. She lives in the Gold Coast neighborhood in Chicago, IL also known as the GOAT urban neighborhood! It is a clean, safe, upscale, and is in the perfect location for her lifestyle. It is right next to the Mag Mile and Oak Street Beach with many dining options, high-end shops and five-star hotels.

Gold Coast is a safe neighborhood. It has many nearby education institutions. It is only a ten-minute drive from downtown, meaning you are in the heart of the city. Everything you need is nearby and accessible. It is close to the lake and the smell of the wind against the lake in the summer is well worth the cost to live in this area. There are many things to do in the neighborhood, including tourist attractions nearby from visiting Millennium Park to walking down Rush Street where there are several places to eat and shop. The night life is incredible with plenty of restaurants and shops nearby. It is also quiet at night, even with such a booming night life.

Why did she leave the sunny city of San Mateo and move to Chicago? It certainly isn't for the weather.

LYDIA SANCHEZ

Intro

Thirty-one years old, five foot, four inches with a slender build. She has long dark brown hair, very well kept. Her makeup is always flawless. When she is not in scrubs, she is wearing designer clothing, jewelry and purses. Lydia wears nothing but the best.

She is an emergency room doctor at Lake Front Memorial Hospital. She lives in Streeterville, in Chicago, Illinois by Lake Michigan. She moved to this area while attending to medical school at Northwestern University. This neighborhood is in the medical district of downtown Chicago and it is close to the

Lakefront and Navy Pier. It's in walking distance of the Loop. This is a safe community, filled with a lot of shopping, restaurants, beautiful architecture, museums, cafes and parks. Streeterville has a neighborhood feel to it and close to high-end stores, which is where she likes to shop.

Lydia is from Bronx, New York and speaks many languages. Her parents are from Portugal where she and her sister were born. Her little sister Luna was born with an enlarged heart, which is the major reasons her parents came to New York to seek medical care for Luna. Her parents came to the states when they were young; in fact, Lydia doesn't remember living any place other than the Bronx.

There are several top medical schools on the East Coast, so what brought her all the way to Chicago from the Bronx

JAMISON HENDRIX

Intro

Thirty years old, six foot, four inches, with broad shoulders and an athletic build. He came to Chicago from Miami, Florida to study robotic engineering in the health care sector at North Western University. He continued to get a master's degree in engineering and biology because he wanted to design surgical instruments and robots. He comes from a very wealthy family; he didn't have to work during college because he could write a check to pay for his education up front. This is how he could maintain a double major of engineering and premed. Jamison is very health conscious. He runs every morning before work, when the Chicago weather permits. He also works out daily in his neighborhood gym, where the ladies hit on him every chance they get. Yes, he is that good looking and charming. He also loves to cook, and he's incredibly good at it.

He lives in the River North Apartments in downtown Chicago on the twentieth floor, his view overlooks the city's skyline. The neighborhood is full of shops and is within walking distance of the business district in the loop where he works. Living in this neighborhood provides endless options to explore, from art galleries, luxury shops, posh night clubs and cocktail bars. It has some of the city's best dining, and this neighborhood is a superb place to live, work and play.

Jamison works at North Shore Robotic Engineering Firm and spends many hours in the ER observing surgical procedures being performed with his designs, which he calls his babies. Jamison works closely with surgeons and hospital administrators designing the tools, instruments and surgical robots to assist in surgeries. The main hospital he works with is Lake Front Memorial. This hospital has an elite surgical team, specializing in organ transplants and oncology. Not only does Jamison love his job and inventions, but he also loves the money he makes to accommodate his lavish lifestyle. Oh, nothing but the best for this gentleman and that is exactly what he is, a charming, educated, good looking gentleman, who enjoys the finer things in life.

So, what would bring him to the Windy City for college and what would make him settle down in Chicago for good?

JADE ALEXANDER

Intro

Thirty years old, five foot five, with a small lean stature, but a big voice. She came to Chicago from Seattle, Washington, to study pre-law at North Western University. After successfully completing her bachelor's degree, she attended University of Chicago Law School, where she received her law degree.

Jade is a corporate lawyer at Stern & Kramer Law Firm. This is a one stop law firm for all your business needs. She is one of the top corporate lawyers, she specializes in leading corporate and financial clients through acquisitions, mergers, and joint ventures. She also councils her clients on business transactions with other entities and advises them about regulations and licensing of new technologies. She manages all legal disputes. She is also the top trademark and patent lawyers in her firm.

Jade is the poster child for dress for success. When she steps out of her condo, she looks like she is ready for the cover of Forbes magazine. Her style is professional business, she dresses for the role she wants to achieve, partner of her law firm with plans to become a judge. When heading to the office, she usually wears her silky black hair pulled back or up in a bun, with classy hair clips.

She lives in the Loop at East Waterside. This is a central area to live in because much of the activity in Chicago happens here. This area is clean, safe and has convenient access to the rest of the city. There is always something to do, from great museums theaters, restaurants, shopping and a fabulous night life. Jade particular loves walking or jogging on the river walk to enjoy the beautiful sights and architecture this city has to offer. This neighborhood has an urban feel to it and it reminds her of her neighborhood back home.

Speaking of back home, what brought her all the way across the country to attend college and law school?

CHAPTER TWO

Friday

VICTORIA

Friday

Ring, "Good morning," Victoria says," How are you this morning Jade?" Jade replied, "Good Morning, I'm fabulous, dear." Jade says, "Hold on, while I get Lydia and Jamison on the phone with us. Good morning Lydia, Jade is on the line, hold on and I will connect us with Jamison." Phone ringing. "This is Jamison!" "We know who this is!" Laughter! "What's up, Ladies!" Victoria says, "Just confirming we are still meeting at the SPOT tonight at eight o'clock to go over the itinerary of our annual vacation." Jade says, "Yes, I will be there." Lydia says, "After a long night in ER last night, I'm looking forward to it, since my vacation actually started at eight o'clock this morning." Jamison replies, "I'm looking forward to it Ladies." Victoria reminds Jade to please bring the brochures and reservation documents. Lydia says, "Outstanding because I need a break from the Windy City like yesterday, and before old man winter arrives. I'm ready to smell the ocean in St. Lucia and run my feet through the warm white sand."

Victoria arrives at the bank with a full agenda for today; including a very important board meeting with the finance committee to discuss the financial statements for the second quarter. As the bank president, she oversees all aspects of the bank's operations and procedures. In this position, she must make decisions in the best interest of the board of directors, employees, customers and federal regulatory institutions. She must also monitor all operations of the bank, to make sure the bank is performing well and all returns on investments are maximized.

Victoria's executive assistant, Bridget Kingston, provides administrative and development support to the president and board of directors. She serves as the primary contact for internal and external constituencies on all matters pertaining to the president. Bridget has a very important role as Victoria's right hand, and Victoria requires excellence from her staff. Bridget has been with Victoria for five years and has always exceeded her expectations in her work performance. She knows the day-to-day functionality of the bank and the bank runs seamlessly when

Victoria is away BUT lately, Bridget has not been the same. Her work has not been stellar, as it has in the past, AND she hasn't been reliable lately. She frequently calls off sick, since her car accident about six months ago. Victoria has significant concern about going out of the country next week, so she has been secretly training the vice president Stewart Newman and Amanda Meeks, the loan manager, how to handle Bridget's task while she is on vacation. They prepared the agenda and reports for this morning's board meeting to get familiar with the financial statements for this branch.

Victoria says to Amanda and Stewart, "Where is she? It's not like her to be late! It's nine twenty and the meeting starts at ten o'clock. Let's get started preparing the conference room for the meeting with the financial packets." As the board members and financial stake holders arrive, Amanda directs them into the conference room and Victoria starts the meeting with introductions and says, "I apologize for the delay as my assistant had an emergency and will not be attending. Stewart will be the acting liaison for today's meeting. He is up to speed and will be the acting interim and Amanda will handle all day-to-day operations along with Bridget while I'm on vacation next week."

"Great meeting," says Mr. Zolner, the senior board member. "The bank is on target to achieve the goals set forth and the financial statements look great! Job well done! Very well done!" Victoria is thinking, *I'm so glad that is over.* She says to Stewart, "I could not think straight in the meeting because I was wondering what happened to Bridget. I don't have any missed calls from her and now I'm very concerned. She has never been a no call, no show in the five years she has worked for me. Something must definitely be wrong." Stewart says, "Calm down Victoria, try calling her cell again."

"Bridget, I've been sick about you. Are you okay?" Bridget says, "Yes, I'm okay. I've been in the emergency room all night and I thought I would be release in time for work. What time is it?" Victoria says, "It's eleven thirty; What happened, why are you in the emergency room?" Bridget replied, "I was very dizzy last night and fell as I was getting out of the shower. My neighbor, Mrs. Joseph, you know the nosy one I was telling you about. The one who lives below me, said she heard the loud bang. She called me and when I didn't answer, she banged on my door and dialed 911. Mrs. Joseph had also contacted the building manager, before the police arrived to gain entry. Upon entry, they found me on the bathroom floor bleeding from my head. I was unconscious, so they called an ambulance, which brought me to Lake Front Memorial. I'm so sorry I didn't call you earlier this morning, but I've been groggy, and my thoughts are so foggy, right now. Victoria says, "Oh, don't you worry about that, I'm just glad you are okay. What are the doctors saying? Do you need me to come to the hospital?" Bridget replies, "I'm fine, and I should get released soon. I just have a colossal headache radiating up the right side of my head, just above my ear. All I can remember, is stepping out of the shower and I slipped. My head must have hit the edge of vanity cabinet. Besides, you have your vacation to get ready for. I will just go home when I'm released and check in with you later this afternoon. I'm sure I will be back to work next week, they only kept me overnight for observation."

Victoria says, "My friend Lydia is a doctor on staff, I can have her check on you." Bridget replies, "Oh, no need for that. I'm feeling much better already, and my sister is here with me. I'm fine Victoria, you have your trip to get ready for and I apologize for not contacting you sooner." Victoria replies, "It's okay; you just take care of yourself and I will see you when I return." Victoria's thoughts are running through her head, *now I feel guilty because I thought she was calling off sick again, with no genuine explanation for her absences. I was ready to take corrective action this time, but the poor thing is really hurt.*

Victoria says, "Well, no time for lunch today, if I want to get out of here on time. With Bridget out, I have a lot to catch Stewart up on. No time to be in vacation mode until after five o'clock today. Look out St. Lucia, here we come!"

LYDIA

Friday

A lady arrived in emergency room via ambulance from a car accident. She sustained traumatic injuries and needs emergency surgery. The paramedics are working hard to get her stabilized. Lydia recognizes this lady from back home in Bronx, New York. She is wondering, *how in the world did she end up in Chicago. That life seems like a lifetime ago. I hope she doesn't recognize me.*

Lydia asked the nurse, "What's the patient's name?" The nurse replies, "We don't know Dr. Sanchez, she didn't have any identification when she arrived. Ben was the paramedic that brought her in. He said the impact of the collision ejected her from the vehicle." Lydia says, "Can you get Ben in here? We need information on her. I need her medical history and I need it right now. Did she have any family with her?" The nurse replies, "No, Dr. Sanchez, she arrived alone. Here comes Ben now. Hey Ben, did this patient have any identification? We need a medical history on her STAT." Ben replies, "No, Dr. Sanchez. When we arrived at the scene, she had been ejected from the vehicle and was unconscious." Lydia says, "Can you please ask the officers if they found any identification or if they have notified any family members? Are there any others here from the accident?" Ben answers, "Yes, there was only one other passenger in the vehicle, she arrived in a different ambulance." Lydia says to the nurse, "Can you ask the officers if anyone in the car had any identification. If they are stable, we will need information on our lady." Lydia is thinking; *I know her full name and her entire family's name, but I can't let anyone know that I know her. It will raise too many questions and I left that life back in the Bronx."*

Patient is crashing! Get the crash cart in here STAT." Lydia starts CPR, then after several rounds of shocking her, she is stable but still unconscious. Lydia orders x-rays and a CT scan to determine if there is any internal bleeding and to assess the head trauma. She is stable for now, but we need to hurry. Lydia is thinking, *I wonder who is with her? I hope they don't recognize me.* She is breathing heavily, the nurse asked if she is okay? "Oh, I'm fine, I just don't want to lose her. I just get a little worked up, when it's a close call." The nurse replies, "I understand Dr. Sanchez, it's what makes you a brilliant doctor." Lydia asked the nurse, "Is the other passenger stable? We really need to find out our Jane Does medical history."

A nurse comes in and says, "That's what I came in to tell you. There was a young lady in the car with our Jane doe and she was rushed to surgery. I have her chart, her name is Maria Ramirez, age twenty-nine, with a broken pelvis, broken femur and deep lacerations to her right thigh. They rushed her to surgery to save her leg." Lydia asked, "Was she conscious when she arrived? Did she say anything?" Nurse Jessica said, "According to Dr. Peters who is treating her, she was asking about her mother, who was in the car with her. He said she kept repeating; she didn't see the other car, it came out of nowhere and slammed into the passenger side, where her mother was sitting. Dr. Peters said, she was in and out of consciousness because of the pain medication he had given her. That is the only information we have." Lydia says to the nurse, "Please let me know when Dr. Peters is out of surgery, we need information on our lady. I will go check on her test results."

Lydia's mind is racing a mile a minute. *Oh, my God! It is them. Why in the world would they be in Chicago? This is not happening. Even if her mom doesn't wake up, Maria will definitely recognize me; we used to run game together; she knows my entire past life, the life I wanted to leave in New York.* Lydia asked the technician, "Do you have the x-rays and CT scan back for our Jane doe?" The technician pulls the film up on the bright screen and says, "Yes, Dr. Sanchez, here are the images and films." Lydia tells the technician to have Dr. Yang paged right away to come and look at the images. Lydia calls the head nurse, and tells her, our Jane doe has a brain bleed on the right side, she needs surgery right away or she will not make it. She then instructs her to get a rush on the labs because we need her blood type right away. To reserve an operating room and to get an anesthesiologist and surgical team for Dr. Yang.

Lydia says, "Dr. Yang, is it as bad as it looks? Can you stop the brain bleed? Her x-rays also show a broken shoulder and several broken ribs along her right side. The driver of the car said our Jane doe was sitting on the passenger side. A car hit them while going through the intersection." After a lengthy pause, and uh-hum-ooh-hmm, from Dr. Yang, he finally says, "Yes, but we have to hurry, do we have any medical history on our Jane doe?" Lydia says, "No, but we have her EKG results, it looks great, and her vital signs are finally stable. I've ordered a rush on her lab work and will have it sent to OR two, I have reserved for you." Dr. Yang says to Lydia, "That's why you are my favorite ER doctor at Lake Front Memorial." He winks his eye at her and heads to OR two.

Lydia asked Dr. Peters how Maria's surgery went. Dr. Peters says, "She is stable for now and as long as her leg doesn't get infected and has continued blood flow, we should be able to save it. The next twenty-four hours will tell." Lydia is happy Maria will keep her leg; and she's even happier, her shift is over in a couple of hours.

JAMISON

Friday

"Good morning Dr. Naomi, are you ready to use the new flex surgical tool today?" Long pause, Dr. Naomi is not one for many words and Jamison has grown accustom to her demeanor over the past five years. He has worked closely with her; designing surgical instruments. Dr. Naomi is very precise with her request, which causes them to work together quite frequently. Dr. Naomi finally answers, "Yes, I'm ready." Jamison asked, "Have you practiced handling the flex robotic tool?" Dr. Naomi gives him a stare and says, "You know better than to ask such. After all, I am the best on this side of the hemisphere." Jamison can relate to her arrogance because he has the same personality, only he is more social and has better mannerism. Jamison changes into scrubs after washing his hands. One of the surgical assistants puts the mask around his face before he entered the surgical area. Dr. Naomi double checked each instrument on the tray to ensure everything is in place. This specially designed flex robotic arm is being used for the first time on a patient and Jamison is excited about it. Dr. Naomi can see his big smile through his dark almond-shaped eyes that are glistering as she uses the tool. Today's procedure is to remove a tumor off the liver of a mid-age patient. Dr. Naomi wanted this design because it would be less evasive for the patient and the patient will have a much faster recovery time. It is also a quicker surgical procedure for her, which means she will be available to do more surgeries per day.

Dr. Naomi says to Jamison, "That was a success, and I completed this procedure in record time. Jamison, you are a genius for this design, I believe this is the best one yet." It surprised Jamison because Dr. Naomi does not give compliments. She will just state, I can use this, or I can use that, or it worked just as I needed it to, but to say Jamison was a genius. *Wow,* he thought. Jamison says to Dr. Naomi, "I'm very pleased that you are happy." She tells Jamison she will have her report of the instrument completed by this afternoon and send it over to North Shore Robotics today. Jamison thanks her as he is exiting the room and says, "Keep your eyes peeled." Dr. Naomi smiles as they always end their time together with this phrase from Jamison. Dr. Naomi tells Jamison to expect a call from Jon today, it's time. Jamison flashes those deep dimples and perfectly straight white teeth and continues to exit.

He is excited and can now concentrate on his upcoming vacation in St. Lucia. What a way to end the work week with a very satisfied top paying client for his firm. Jamison can't wait to get out of those cotton scrubs and back into his tailor-made Italian suit. On his way out of the hospital, he receives a call on is cell phone from an unknown number. He answers "This is..." He pauses for a minute, the caller says, "Jamison, this is Jon, we need to meet today." Jamison replies, "What number are you calling from? This is not the number I have for you." Jon replied, "This is my business cell number, lock it in your phone. What time can we meet?" Jamison says, "It will have to be early afternoon because I have evening plans and my flight leaves early Sunday morning." Jon says, "That's why I need to meet with you in person today, to discuss what we talked about the other night." Jamison says, "Let's meet at two o'clock at the same spot as last week, the Windsor on East Huron Street. Jon agrees and says, "Remember what I said Jamison, If you are not willing to risk the usual, you will have to settle for the ordinary." Jamison ends the call with "Keep your eyes peeled."

He is toying with the conversation that just ended. He is contemplating this business proposition, but he hasn't made a final decision yet. Although he trusts Dr. Naomi, he is not sure about Jon. Jamison heads to his firm to complete his report from this morning's procedure, then to the gym, before his meeting with Jon this afternoon.

JADE

Friday

Jade is at the office, sitting at her desk that overlooks the city's skyline. Her office has high ceilings and very large windows. She has big beautiful walnut office furniture. Her desk is a Stovall Executive desk, it is oval with a curvy shape, all corners are rounded and seem to wrap around and hug you when you are sitting behind it. The scales of justice is sitting on her desk, with the gravel sitting next to it. This is something she has wanted to achieve since she was a little girl and she is very proud of her accomplishments. There is a small oval shaped conference table with four conference room style chairs in the far corner by the large windows. Her office has a built-in bookshelf that encases the entire wall.

Jades phone rings, "Yes Sandy," she answers. Sandy says, "Mr. Stern would like to see you this morning. I see you have a ten o'clock open. Will this be a good time to meet with him?" Jade answer, "Yes, but what is the meeting about?" Sandy says, "I'm not sure, I was only asked to confirm your schedule for today and if ten o'clock is fine, then the meeting will be in conference room C." Jade answers, "I will be there." Jade is wondering *what in the world is this all about. My clients are happy, and I've brought on new accounts this quarter, I haven't lost any cases in court in over a year, so I wonder what this is all about?* Although Jade is very successful and confident in the office, her personal self-confidence is at the bottom of the scale. She has this inner battle with herself, second guessing her decisions; just to confirm later, it was the best choice. She puts herself through turmoil, trying to find an error or catch a mistake. She is very uptight, when it comes to her career and always assumes the partners are looking for a way to get rid of her. She has the heaviest case load and put in more hours than any of the other attorneys at the firm. She is not the only female, so she can't say, it's because she is not part of the good ole boys' club. Jade sets her watch alarm to vibrate at nine forty-five, since conference room C is on the other side of the building.

Buzz, her watch vibrates, her heart pumps fast as she reaches for her notebook and heads down the long hallway. She enters the conference room, which is very elegant with a modern hanging crystal chandelier that looks like something you would see in the entryway of a mansion. The high back black leather chairs are so plush, it feels like you are sitting on foam. She looks around the room and Mr. Stern, and Mr. Kramer are both sitting at the conference room table. Now her heart beats even faster, because this is her first-time meeting with both since she interviewed for the job four years ago. "Come on in and have a seat," says Mr. Stern. His assistant Sandy enters right behind her. Jade addresses them both, "Good morning, Mr. Stern and Mr. Kramer," as she takes a seat. Mr. Kramer starts off by saying, "Jade, you have worked for us about four years now, right?" *Jade says to herself, well, you should know I'm sure you have my file in front of you and I'm sure you two had already discussed this before setting up this meeting.* Jade replies, "Yes, that is correct." Silence, as Sandy types on her laptop. Jade has learned, over the years, to wait for the first person to speak and watch their body language. Mr. Kramer says, "Jade we have brought you in here, because we have a big account we just received, and we would like for you to take it on. Now, we will provide you with a team to assist you and you can use them and delegate some of your other workload. We want you to focus on this big account." Mr. Stern pops in and says, "It's the Lake Front Memorial Hospital account, we want to you to be the legal counsel for us. This could make you a partner sooner than planned." Jade's body language shifts from defense mode to a curious mode, she leans forward, smiles, and exclaimed, "Thank you sir, this is huge! I really appreciate this opportunity and I will not disappoint you." They hand her the files and start going over a few details. Mr. Stern then says, "We understand you are on vacation next week, but we were hoping you would take the files with you to be up to speed on the open litigations when you return. Sandy will email you the digital file so you can review them, while sitting by the ocean." He makes a half-crooked smile; Jade knows this is not a if you have the time; it is expected for her to make time. Jade answers, "Yes sir, I will be up to speed when I return." They end the meeting with a handshake and exit the conference room.

Jade doesn't know if she wants to scream with excitement or be pissed off, this was dropped on her, the last day, before her vacation. She is thinking, *now I will have to take work along with me, which is against our vacation rules. I will have to just explain to them, I will have to work a few hours of each day.*

Buzz, Jade's watch goes off. It's time to go home and get ready to meet the gang for dinner at the SPOT tonight.

CHAPTER THREE
THE SPOT

Friday Night

The BLVD is an American cuisine restaurant and bar in Chicago's West Loop neighborhood, that reminds you of Hollywood's Sunset Blvd in the 1950's. It was known as the playground for the stars. The BLVD has the old Hollywood glamour that has a mix of contemporary cuisine, cocktails and music. Creating a unique blend between the vintage past and the vibrant present. This restaurant serves not only American food but also foods from around the globe. BLVD offers an internationally inspired spread of re-invented classic dishes, rooted in different cuisines and cultures. It holds three hundred people and has private rooms to reserve for private events. The Champagne Room seats up to sixty people and can host a standing reception for up to eighty-five people. It has a private bar and a full television and audiovisual capabilities. The Gallery has a semi-private space that seats up to forty people and can host standing receptions for up to fifty people.

This place is classy with elegance. It has two levels with a wide winding staircase, encased in dark wood. The walls are textured, and beige. The floors and tabletops are walnut wood with beige colored crush velvet chairs. Some dinner seating has large round metallic colored seating and some walls are a deep purple. The lights are dim with long modern crystal hanging chandeliers about four feet from the ceilings on the upper level the windows are round shaped like what you see on a cruise ship. The bar has studio lighting over glass shelves, that hold various liquors that overtake the entire wall, pure elegance.

This place is enormous, you could easily get lost in the crowd and your friend or spouse wouldn't know you were even there. That's why Jamison calls it the SPOT! The dress code in the evening is formal. Oh, and there is also valet parking, if you need it.

Jade arrives first at eight twenty. She is wearing an after five off-white party dress, with slender straps and a plunging neckline to highlight her luminous skin. Her shoes, a pointy toe pump with a liquid-shine of white patent leather, made by Steve Madden. She is carrying a clutch that matches her shoes with a gold chain strap. She has on pearl stud earrings and a pearl necklace. She wears one ring on her left middle finger, it's leaf shaped gold tone pearl ring with diamonds surrounding it. Jade is classy and simple at the same time. Victoria had made reservations for the Ellis' party of four, so getting seated was not a problem, not to mention, they were all regulars, some more than others! "Ellis' party come this way please" says the hostess. Jade sits at one of the round metallic tables. She takes the plane tickets, pamphlets, reservations, brochures and itineraries and places them around the table as places settings so everyone can review it upon being seated.

Victoria arrives next. She is wearing a black sequin bodice long sleeve jumpsuit by Vince Camuto. It has a jewel trimmed neckline, fitted to show off her petite waist. Her shoes are, pointy toed pump made by Jeffrey Campbell, covered with tiny crystals and a hint of turquoise underneath. These shoes make a statement when they enter the room. She is carrying a clutch which matches her shoes. Victoria is wearing a silver turquoise ring on her right middle finger that catches your eye. She says, "Hello dear how was your day?" Jade replies, "All I can say is, Thank God it's Friday." Victoria retorts, "I can relate because I had one of those days myself. I will share it with you, while I'm drinking my apple martini."

Lydia arrives, and this fashion diva is wearing a vintage inspired cocktail dress illuminated with a multitude of glittering dots. The dress is knee-length with a flowing lacy hem. It is off the shoulder and has cap sleeves. The dress has a fitted leather waistline to accentuate her petite figure. She is wearing hazel pointy toe snake skinned pumps, made by Sam Edelman. She is carrying a Fendi medium black clutch with a long gold chain strap. Her earrings are fourteen karat gold with diamond hoops by Dana Rebecca Designs. She has an oval shaped black onyx ring on her left pinky finger and a thick black and gold bracelet on the left arm. "Hey ladies, are we ready to get out of the city or what? I had one of the worse nights ever last night and I need straight whiskey this evening!" Jade and Victoria looked at each other and laughed. Lydia says, "What's so funny? Yes, I said whiskey!" Then she laughed. No has taken their orders yet, which is surprising because they are regulars. "It's eight twenty-six and where is Jamison?" says Jade. "He is never this late, in fact, I was expecting him to be here before I arrived." Jamison's philosophy is five minutes early is late, which he never was.

Eight thirty on the nose. Here comes Jamison walking over to the table with a drink in his hand and a big smile on his face, flashing his deep dimples. "Hello Ladies!" This guy is so smooth. He is wearing a navy-blue Johnston Lenin suit with a tan and caramel striped shirt; his necktie is navy blue with caramel stripes. His shoes are Timmons wingtip lace up style, burnished dark brown calfskin. His is wearing a Sea-Dweller Rolex watch with a pewter and gold finish on his left wrist. His right hand has a Versace Medusa ring on the ring finger. His right wrist has a silver and gold intertwined chain link bracelet. He wears Bleu De Chanel cologne. The scent is a woody, aromatic fragrance for the man who defies convention. They infuse this cologne with crisp citrus notes and offer an intense concentration of the fresh, clean, vibrant fragrance, which is unexpected and undeniably bold. You can smell Jamison well after he has left the room.

As he slides into the round booth, of course, on the end, he says, "How was your day Ladies?" Everyone moans, which is unusual because they love what they do, and they each have successful careers. Jamison jerks back his left shoulder and says, "Whaatt? This is not like you ladies. Now someone had to have had a good day besides me." as he flashes those perfect white teeth. Jade was thinking, he was looking especially smooth tonight.

The server comes over to take their drink orders. Lydia and Victoria look over the itinerary. Jade announces, as they brought the drinks to the table, "We can go over the itinerary together." The server comes back with drinks and says, "Apple martin!" Victoria motions him to place the drink in front of her. "Whisky Neat for the gentleman," Lydia motions him to place it in front of her and immediately orders a second one. "Chardonnay?" He places it in front of Jade. Jamison orders another whiskey neat.

Victoria says, "Okay, now that we all have our drinks, let's go over the itinerary, I've been waiting for months to see what Jade planned for us and I'm so ready for this vacation." Jade picks up the flight schedule and says, "Our flight departs Sunday morning from O'Hare airport at five forty on American Airlines. Here are your e-tickets, I printed them out for you all. We have a one hour and fifteen-minute layover in Atlanta. Then our last flight to St. Lucia, arrives at two fifteen in the afternoon. We will have approximately a fifty-minute taxi ride from the airport to the Calabash Cove Resort. This year I picked an all-inclusive resort so we will not have to share the amenities with children. Each of you have a brochure of the resort and a brochure of the attractions, I reserved for us. They each look at the information and nod their head in unison. Victoria says, "This is fabulous Jade! As always, you never disappoint us with the vacation plans." Jade blurts out, "Well, my workload has intensified, so one of you will handle next year's vacation plans." Everyone grabs their adult beverage in silence. Jade has been the one to plan the annual vacation every year since college. It all started with the first spring break and no one could decide where they wanted to go. Jade decided the only way they would actually go on a trip was if she planned it herself. Jade so desperately wants one of them to take on the task next year, or even for a couple of years at that.

The server comes back to the table with Lydia's and Jamison's second drink. Victoria orders another apple martini. The server asked, "Is anyone having dinner tonight?" Victoria replied, "Sure, but can you give us a few more minutes, please?" They are very excited about the amenities and the resort. Victoria reads, "Nestled on a lush, tropical hillside sloping gently towards the turquoise waters of the Caribbean Sea. Calabash cove takes romance to new levels with a secluded white sand beach and a custom-designed boardwalk that's perfect for candlelit dinners or romantic sunset strolls. The resort's charming and unique accommodations include handcrafted teak and mahogany Water Edge Cottages right on the beach, also swim-up suites, and ocean view junior suites. All accommodations feature private Jacuzzis and many offer private plunge pools, hammocks and outdoor rain showers." Everyone smiles, Jade continues.

"Jamison requested the Water's Edge Cottage with pool, with the outdoor rain shower and hammocks. It's on the water's edge, surrounded by its own tropical flora with a view across the bay. We each have our very own Sunset Junior Suite that has balcony views of the Mosaic Beach and the Caribbean Sea." They tease Jamison about why he needed a private pool and outdoor rain shower? They giggle like they did when they were in college. Jamison flashes his perfect white teeth and says, "Keep your eyes peeled," then he says to Jade, "I really appreciate you planning this. I know that you are as busy, if not busier, as the rest of us. Just know that we do not take all that you do for granite. Lydia finally says something, "I think this is the best vacation yet, let's all toast to Jade and twelve years of friendship."

They order dinner and have a couple more drinks, the band is playing jazz. They sit with their eyes closed in silence. They are just listening to the music, popping their fingers to the beat, and singing the lyrics out loud, just enjoying each other's company in their favorite spot. Finally Jade says, "Oh, we didn't go over the activities I reserved for us." Victoria says, "We can get the details when we get there or on the plane, but right now, don't disturb this groove." Jamison and Lydia lift their glass to show they agree.

The band took a short intermission and Jade said to Jamison, "I didn't see you come in. Have you been here a while?" Jamison says, "Yes, I met a colleague in the Champagne Room around six thirty for a private event." Victoria asked, "What kind of event?" Jamison says, "New possibilities!" with a big smile. Victoria replied, "New possibilities?" They laugh. Lydia asked Jade, how much do they owe her for the plane tickets? Jade replied, "Nothing! Jamison paid for them." Then they looked at Jamison and said, "You paid for our airfare?" Jamison said, "It was bonus money for my new surgical tool. It was a great success and since the bonus was for more than I imagined; I thought I would bless my friends with airfare." Lydia exclaimed, "Let's toast to Jamison."

The server comes with their food, Jamison ordered the sixteen-ounce New York Strip with a side of brussels sprouts with red pepper coulis, guanciale, a baked potato, and a glass of spring water. Victoria ordered a sixteen-ounce Pork Chop, with a side of roasted cauliflower chimichurri; she also has sparking water with her meal. Jade ordered an eight-ounce Filet Mignon with a side of mixed mushrooms and baked potato. She orders another glass of Chardonnay with her meal. Lydia ordered Carolina Gold rice maitake mushrooms, mixed vegetables with cashew butter, black truffle with a side of roasted cauliflower chimichurri. She orders another whiskey neat.

Jamison look at Lydia and gently says, "You are really hitting the whiskey hard tonight Lydia." She softly replied, "It was a rough night in the ER last night and I'm so glad I have next week off." Jamison asked, "Did you lose a patient?" Lydia nods her head slowly, then said. "We had multiple car accidents. Four people are in critical condition. Six gunshot victims arrived and were rushed to surgery. Two heart attack victims, one came in by ambulance, the other by car and eight people decided to overdose." Jamison says to Lydia, "A night like that, I got your next drink."

Jade says, "And I thought my workload was bad. The partner of my firm dumped a new account on me today. They expect me to be up to speed and prepared when I return. So, don't give me any crap because I have to review this account while on vacation." They look over at Victoria who was fishing for her green olive at the bottom of her martini glass, Jamison says, "And you? I know you had to have some drama at the bank this week." Victoria says, "Yes, it's that darn Bridget again, she called off sick today. We had a board meeting to go over our financial statements and bank performance. I'm glad I had already trained Amanda and Stewart as a backup, while I'm on vacation next week." Jade asked, "What's her story this time?" With a frown on her face. Victoria says, "I was getting ready to take corrective action this time, but the poor thing ended up at Lake Front Memorial with a head injury. She fell getting out of the shower and was taken in by ambulance." Lydia immediately says, "When was this? I can make a call to confirm if she was really there." Jamison says, "Right now ladies, let's just focus on our vacation and spending time together. You can validate her story when you return. Let's enjoy this night and start preparing tomorrow for our departure on Sunday morning." Victoria says to Jamison, "And I guess you had a great day today?" Jamison says, "Well, let's just say I had a successful surgical demonstration this morning. The hospital is going to buy my new flex surgical tool."

Victoria said, "Let's toast to Jamison, and his big win." Jade says, "I'm so proud of you," as she gives him a warm smile. This is all you talked about when you first started engineering school twelve years ago, a hospital buying your designs and using it to help the world." Lydia exclaims, "Look at us, we are living our dreams. Twelve years ago, it seemed so far away, and now here we are.

Jade says, "Let's toast to our success and how we pushed forward despite the hard times we had getting here. Victoria, a successful bank president. Jade, a successful corporate attorney, soon make partner." Jamison says, "And you Lydia, a successful emergency room doctor and surgeon. Looks like all of those years of hard work and sacrifice paid off." Victoria replies, "Yes, we made it and I don't think I would have made it, if I didn't have good friends like you." Jamison says, "We are not friends, we are family, and don't you forget it."

They order another round of drinks. The music is more upbeat now and they are rocking in their seat. Lydia says, "No more talk about work, we are celebrating twelve years of friendship and what God has joined together let no man put asunder." They each chime in to finish the quote in unison.

They are looking at each other and thinking to themselves, *if you only knew what I had to do to get to this point in my life; If you only knew what I did in my past; If you only knew the family matters, I left back home; If you only knew what I'm about to say yes to.* They continue to enjoy the great music and more drinks.

CHAPTER FOUR

The Morning After

VICTORIA

The Morning After

"Oh my! What was I thinking to have that many martinis last night? My head is exploding." She looks over at the clock, it says noon. She jumps out of bed and screams inside. How could I have slept so long? I have a million things to do get ready for vacation tomorrow morning. I do not know why Jade booked those darn flights so early? I didn't want to complain, since I did not have to pay for the airfare. I didn't want to sound ungrateful last night. She looks for her purse to find her cell phone and discovers an ATM receipt from the casino. She says, "How did this get in my purse? I don't remember going to the casino after I left the SPOT last night." She logs in to her online bank account to check her balance and discovers she withdrew three thousand dollars last night. She checks her wallet and says, "I had to win something, I'm sure. I know I did not lose three thousand dollars. I just had a two-thousand-dollar loss on Wednesday night. That's five grand in a few days?" She says out loud as if she were scolding herself, "That's it! "I'm finished with gambling. This is foolish to lose five grand in two days." She starts the shower in disgust while thinking, *I'm glad I have a large savings account, or I would be in trouble. Heck, I spent my mortgage money in two days. I know I always say, a watched penny never breeds, but I better put my pennies on a leach.*

Victoria's condo is at Fifteen Fifty on the Park at the intersection of three celebrated Chicago neighborhoods, Gold Coast, Lincoln Park, and Old Town. The thirty-two-signature residence at 1550 N. Clark Street over looks Lincoln Park, Lake Michigan, and the Chicago skyline. This building only has four units per floor, which enhances privacy by providing intimate and quiet spaces. Her condo has two bedrooms with a den and two full bathrooms. This luxurious space is two thousand, four hundred and seventy-seven square feet and has a private balcony that is four hundred and fourteen square feet. She uses her den as her home office. The condo has an open floor plan with a chef inspired luxury kitchen and high-end appliances. The kitchen cabinetry is custom made with a walnut finish, two stainless steel wall ovens, along with a stainless-steel dishwasher and refrigerator. The island separates the kitchen from the main living room made of natural stone and custom walnut cabinetry. The condo has white oak hardwood floors throughout, except for the bedrooms.

The master suite has a gracious walk-in-closet. The windows are floor to ceiling that overlook the city. The bedroom color pallet is champagne. The master bathroom has natural wood cabinetry with two floating under-mount sinks and marble counter tops. An oversized corner Jacuzzi tub and a floor to ceiling shower with six shower heads encased in glass. There is a wall mounted floating shower bench that runs along the length of the shower. The high ceilings have recess lighting that reflects the water and earth elements. The decor is like a clean tropical spa with greenery and colorful flowers. There is a big oversized bronze round contemporary chair, in the opposite corner of the tub. The guest bathroom has all the same features without the Jacuzzi bathtub and on a smaller level.

You can view the outdoor area from the main living area and master bedroom through the floor to ceiling windows. The balcony is furnished with sleek contemporary furniture. It has a cozy feel to it because of the large tall green potted plants in each corner. Victoria spends a great deal of time out here when the weather permits.

She finishes her shower and her phone rings from an unknown caller, "Hello, this is Victoria." The caller hung up. She assumes the caller has the wrong number and continues getting dresses for the day. She goes into the kitchen and looks in the fridge for leftovers from last night. She wouldn't dare cook and dirty up her beautiful kitchen. After sniffing several containers, she doesn't find any current ones safe to eat from. She grabs a granola bar out of the cabinet and makes a pot of coffee. She loves the smell of the aroma as it fills her condo. Victoria pulls out her packing list to make sure they packed everything. For the first time, she used Jamison's service and hired someone to do all her packing. She is very pleased with the service. One thing she has learned from Jamison, is how to delegate. She pours the coffee and takes the cup into her bedroom, then turns on the radio to relaxes a bit. The radio is playing old school love songs. The songs bring back memories of her first love back home. She realizes how much she still loves him, even all these years later. She sheds a tiny tear, tells herself to snap out of it. That was then, and this is now. She looks around at her condo and is thinking about her success and how she did it all by herself. It was her best friends who encouraged her along the path to success and how she didn't need her parents to approve or disapprove. How she showed them and showed them well. A more upbeat song comes on and she dances around her beautiful condo and realizes she has so much free time left in her day, thanks to Jamison's referral. She is feeling pretty good. She stops dancing abruptly and remembers she has to transfer money from her savings account to her checking account.

Victoria still can't believe she lost that amount of money this past week, so now she can't go shopping for anything new, to take on vacation tomorrow. Her belly growls, and she realizes that granola bar was a joke. *It's time to get some solid food in my stomach.* She skims the menus in her kitchen junk drawer and decides none of that looks appealing. She decides to pay Jamison a surprise visit. It's been a while since she's had his good home cooking. She's thinking, *this man has some secret ingredients he orders from the Caribbean Island, that he cooks with and it like nothing I've ever had before.* She takes an Uber to his place to avoid the parking hassle.

LYDIA

The Morning After

Lydia is feeling horrible from drinking whiskey last night. The sun is shining big and bright through the sixteenth floor large window of her bedroom. There is nothing worse than a hangover and the sun greeting you when you open your eyes. Lydia didn't know if she had died and was waking up to her new destiny or if she was having a nightmare. Soon she discoverers it was real because her head was banging so hard, she could hardly lift it off the pillow. Her phone rings, it's Jade in her chipper tone, "Hey girl, want to go on a run today." Lydia replies, "Hell no! my head hurts so bad, I can't believe I'm able to speak right now."

Jade laughs and says, "The way you were slamming those whiskey neat's back last night, I thought you were on a suicide mission." They both laugh and Jade says, "I think your nickname will be whiskey-neat." Jade lets out a belly laugh, and Lydia just moans and says, "Not funny and goodbye; I don't want to talk to you again until we get to St. Lucia tomorrow." Jade hangs up laughing even louder.

Lydia practically crawled off her pillow top mattress and nearly fell when her feet hit the floor. The sun was still glowing in her face as she staggered into the bathroom. As she is sitting on the toilet, she looked around her beautiful bathroom with twelve-foot ceilings and recess ceiling lighting. Blue-gray vertical striped walls with gleaming granite counter tops, walnut framed mirrors, Jacuzzi tub, walk-in shower room with over-sized shower head, fluffy towels neatly arranged, the tile floor has an oversized shag rug. A colorful wicker laundry basket sits in the corner. The marble countertop has a white vase with greenery and white lilies.

She ran bathwater, thinking about the events that had taken place the last few days; especially her Thursday night shift in emergency room. Although she tried to drink her worries away last night, they all came back to haunt her even more today. She says out loud, "Snap out of it Lydia, and stop overreacting, it's time to get in vacation mode." Lydia goes to her bathroom medicine cabinet and swallows three Tylenols for the massive headache. Lydia turns on the radio and listens to jazz music while she is soaking in her Jacuzzi tub, filled with bath salts. As she relaxes, she reminisces about her past life and where she is now, a tear falls down her cheek. She can remember when she and her family had nothing, absolutely nothing, and now she is living in a luxury sky rise condo on the sixteenth floor, two bedroom, two full bathrooms; with hardwood floors throughout.

The condo has an open floor plan with floor to ceiling windows and panoramic views of Navy Pier. The kitchen has top of the line stainless steel appliances and walnut wood cabinetry. Her living room has an all-white color pallet with a hint of teal and beige. The same color scheme is throughout the condo, except the guest bedroom and bathroom, have a hint of yellow and teal.

She is thinking about all her accomplishments and how she can lose everything if Maria or Mrs. Ramirez discovers, she was the attending physician when they arrived in ER the other night. She says out loud, "I could lose all of this in the blink of an eye."

Lydia gets out of the tub, dripping wet, reaches for a towel and her phone rings. All kinds of thoughts were going through her mind as she looks at the caller ID. It was an unknown caller. She hesitates and think, maybe I should let it go to voice mail and she does just that. She decided she would retrieve the message after she get dressed and grab a bite to eat. She goes to her massive closet that opens into what seems like a small bedroom and pulls out a blue fitted dress and a pair of tan-colored ankle boots. She lets her long black hair hang down her back, finishes her attire with silver jewelry and accessories; everything designer, you know. She changes purses from last night because the black Fendi doesn't match today's outfit. But when she transfers items from the black clutch to her oversized tan Michael Kors purse, she discovers a name and phone number written on a napkin. It said Sam 312-888-4721. She says out loud, "How did this get in here and who is Sam?" She then remembers sitting at the bar alone last night after the others went home, and different men trying to hit on her but it is not like her to take a number or give hers out. Lydia comes across as the snooty type and gives off the energy that says don't even try it. Now she is seriously thinking about that unknown caller. Could it have been this mysterious Sam?

She leaves to get lunch, while on the elevator, she is contemplating if she should walk since there are so many choices in the neighborhood, with great restaurants within walking distance of her condo. Since it's a beautiful day, it would be refreshing, and she could clear her head. Plus, she didn't want the Saturday afternoon Chicago traffic to irritate her; especially with her hangover from last night. She stops at a Korean restaurant in her neighborhood where she frequently eats. She orders Noodle Stir Kai, one of her usual dishes, a stir-fry sensation created with noodles, spinach, sun-dried tomatoes, grilled onions and mushrooms, with a hit of sesame oil and ginger spice. She orders a hot tea to drink with her meal.

As she is waiting for her meal, she is sipping her tea and

thinking about the phone number from her purse and the name Sam. She finally listens to her voice mail. "Hello beautiful, I hope you are having a wonderful day, this is Sam. I was hoping to catch you and invite you to dinner before you left for your vacation tomorrow morning. Please call me if you would like to have dinner with me this evening. My number is 312-888-4721." She can't believe this guy with the sexy voice and sexy accent knows about her vacation plans. She ponders, "Did I tell a perfect stranger I was going on vacation?"

The server brings her food, and she is no longer hungry because the message and the sexy voice has her distracted. Her stomach growls loudly, and she suddenly remembers why she is there in the first place, and that is to feed her massive hangover. The food and warm tea made her feel so much better and she is now energized. These are the exact nutrients her body needed. After she left the restaurant, she stopped by her favorite smoothie shop and orders a Pure Recharge Mango Strawberry smoothie with multivitamins. She knows she needs to restore her cells after drinking all of that whiskey last night. She is thinking, *speaking of last night, I need to call this Sam with the sexy voice when I make it back to my condo.*

She feels like herself again and now refreshed as she sips on her smoothie. So, she does some window shopping, just taking in the fresh air and sunshine as the wind blows through her long black hair. Being cooped up in ER for twelve hours can really make you appreciate fresh air. The thought of work made her immediately think about Maria Ramirez and her mother. Lydia went into panic mode all over again and walks back towards her building quickly as if someone was following her. As she enters her building, she checks her mailbox, retrieves her mail and gets on the elevator. The elevator ride seems unusually long today. Sixteen floors seemed like twenty-four floors. But it was just the heavy things weighing on her mind that made the elevator ride seem so long.

She enters her apartment and realizes how much of the day she has lost from sleeping in too late. She remembers she needs to pack and prepare for the early flight in the morning. She grabs her iPad and pulls up her packing list she had made two weeks ago. She goes to her hall closet to pull out her large suite case. Her trip is six nights and seven days, so she needs to have plenty of clothing, but more importantly, she needs a suite case big enough for all the items and clothing she would bring back. She takes about two hours to gather all the articles of clothing, jewelry, accessories, shoes, handbags and toiletries and pack them neatly in her suite case. She is now all packed and in vacation mode again.

Her phone rings again and this time it is Victoria, "Hey Lydia, how are you feeling today?" laughter, Lydia replies, "Pretty good, thank you! What's so darn funny?" Victoria says, "Girl, you were putting those whiskey neat's back last night, and then you were going on about a lady and her daughter coming in the ER in critical condition from a terrible car accident. And how you didn't know if the mother would pull through or not? We have never seen you drink like that, Ms. I'm only putting healthy things in my body. How does that body feel today after all those whiskeys neat's?" laughter, Lydia says, "Yes, it was a very tough night. Although I am an experienced doctor and surgeon, sometimes it gets me down. I feel terrible, when people come in mangled, and or damaged beyond our abilities to fix them. Or the worst-case scenario; when they die. It's heartbreaking to see human life in this state." Victoria says softly, "That's why you are the best ER doctor at Lake Front Memorial. You are truly, walking in your calling."

Lydia asked Victoria, "Did I say anything else about the mother and daughter car crash victims?" Victoria says, "No! just that they reminded you of someone back home." Lydia changes the subject and asked, "Are you packed yet?" Victoria replies, "The agency packed me a few days ago. You know how I roll." Lydia says, "Oh, I forgot who I asked that question, *Ms. Time management.*" They chuckle, Victoria says, "Well, I was just checking on you and I see that all is well. I will see you at three thirty in the morning at the airport." Lydia says, "I wouldn't trade it for all the tea in China." They hang up.

Lydia is all packed and decides to return Sam's call. She pulls out the napkin from the SPOT and as she began to dial the number, her phone rings in her hand, it startles her, she answers. "Hello beautiful, this is Sam."

JAMISON

The Morning After

Fifteen, sixteen, seventeen, eighteen, nineteen, twenty, and he relaxes and makes a long sigh. A young man he sees frequently in the gym, walks over to him and says, "Dang man, you are hitting the weights hard this morning!" Jamison raises up, off the bench press and smiles. He walks over to the shoulder press and starts his repetitions. The gentleman follows him and ask, "Have you ever thought about being a personal trainer?" Jamison looks at him with a puzzled and annoyed look and says, "Naw man! I'm busy and I don't have time to be any body's personal trainer. It's a sacrifice for me to work out daily, but I do it because I care about my health and I like to look good for the ladies," as he smiles and nods his head. The young man replied, "Well can I just work out with you from time to time?" Now it annoys Jamison and he replies, "I don't mean to be rude, young blood, but I enjoy working out alone. It's my time to clear my head and work things out in my mind. I have a very stressful job, so this my way to work things out in my head." Then Jamison says, "You know how they make business deals on the golf course, young blood? Well, I make my deals and decisions in the gym. I hope you can respect that." The young man says, "Yes, I can respect that, I will see you around sometime, have a good day."

Jamison felt bad for brushing the young man off, but he doesn't like a lot of unnecessary chatter and non-sense talking. He is a man of very few words, but when he speaks, his words penetrate the soul. He is somewhat a mysterious man, and he likes it this way. He likes to keep everyone wondering where they stand with him. His good looks and perfect white teeth softened his personality. Otherwise, you would think he was a jerk.

Jamison enters the men's' dressing room and on his way there, he stops at the fuel bar and grabs a high protein chocolate smoothie made with dates, nonfat milk, dairy whey blend, almonds, one hundred percent cocoa, whey protein with a blend of antioxidants, vitamins, minerals and phytonutrients for immune support. Now this is not just your ordinary gym, it's a private gym which is more like a private country club. Members do not have to bring anything. They have their own private lockers, fresh warm towels, hot-tubs, Jacuzzi, steam rooms, saunas, private lounge and flat screen televisions along the walls in each dressing room. As Jamison showers, his mind retorts back to his conversations with Dr. Naomi and Jon this past week. He's thinking, *what a heavy load to put on my mind right before I leave for vacation. This vacation is for me to rest and re-group so I can come up with a new robotic surgical invention. I use this time every year to unwind, release all of last year's stresses, and return to the city a refreshed man. It's like coming back recharged and unstoppable, but now I have this huge decision to make that will entirely change my life's path.*

He finishes his shower, gets dressed, shaves and puts on his tailor-made tan slacks and a starched light blue shirt, tan shoes and dabs his Gucci cologne on each side of his neck and on both wrists. He then adds his watch, bracelet, cuff links, and other accessories. He grabs his tan suede jacket and as he prepares to exit the men's dressing room, his cell phone rings. It's Jade, he answers, "What up lady?" She says, "Oh, just finishing up my packing, and I was getting ready to grab a bite to eat. What is your day comprised of?" Jamison says, "Just tying up a few loose ends here in the city and was about to do the same." Jade says, "You mean you didn't have someone come and pack for you this time?" With a snicker. Jamison says, "Of course I did, you know I believe in delegating. That's what successful people do. It leaves me with more time to be innovative. If you weren't so cheap, you could free up a lot of your time and stop trying to be wonder woman." Jade says, "You know my friend, I just may have to take you up on that when we return from vacation because my workload has increased and I'm trying to make partner. This will mean long hours and a lot of weekends at the office to stay on top of things." Jamison says, "You mentioned that last night. How did that happen and who is this new client that will have you so busy?" She said, "My new client is Lake Front Memorial Hospital." Jamison says, "Is that right!" Jade says, "My boss assigned the entire hospital to me to represent the firm." Jamison says, "Jade, this is huge! Congratulations, this could make you a partner." Jade says, "Yes it could, but it was just dropped in my lap yesterday and I will have to go over some files while on vacation, so I'm prepared when I return to the city next week. I know I'm breaking our rules of no work while on vacation, but this is very important to me and I really don't have a choice." Jamison says, "I understand, and so will Lydia and Victoria. You do what you need to do to be ready for this account when we return." Jade felt a heavy load lift off her chest. She says to Jamison, "That's why I'm so blessed to have you as my best friend. You always know how to encourage me, and you always keep it real." Jamison ends the call with, "Keep your eyes peeled, see you in the morning."

By this time, Jamison enters his building at River North Luxury Apartment, his doorman greets him, "Hello Mr. Hendrix." Jamison smiles and says, "It's Jamison, my dad is Mr. Hendrix."

The doorman says, "Very well sir, I mean Jamison." Jamison's mind is so distracted with heavy thoughts of the conversations with Dr. Naomi and Jon this week, he didn't notice Victoria sitting in the lobby. Victoria yells, "Jamison," as he approaches the elevator. Jamison looked like a deer in headlights and says, "Victoria, is everything ok?" She says, "Everything is just fine, I wanted to come hang out with you for a couple of hours." Jamison says, "Hum, we will be together for an entire week starting tomorrow, don't give me that crap. You want me to cook for you, don't you?" He let out a big smile and Victoria nods her head and smiles back at him, like a little girl receiving a new doll. Jamison's says, "Well come on, let's get this party started." They get on the elevator and head to the twentieth floor. Victoria knows that Jamison never talks much on elevators. He only exchanges general greeting and gestures with other tenants and guest of the building.

The elevator opens to the twentieth floor, and they walk towards Jamison's apartment. As Victoria enters, she takes in a big deep breath and says, "I always love coming to your place," Jamison says, "No you like my cooking and that is the only time you visit." They laugh and Victoria says, "You know how busy our lives have become as we have become seasoned in our careers. But you are right, I do love your cooking and you already know, I'm not one to cook." Jamison says, "You designed that big fancy kitchen, with top of the line appliances and cookware and you never used it." Victoria says, "You know it's all for show and besides, I had to have it luxurious since I have an open floor plan like yours." Jamison says, "You mean you got your inspiration from mine!" They laughed.

Victoria notices his new furniture and says, "I love the new design and layout. When did you get new furniture? What happened to that Von Sway room designer you paid all of that money?" She waves her fingers in the air and says, "Were you not feeling the energy?" And let out a belly laugh. Jamison gives her the look and says, "Let's just say, I wasn't feeling the vibe or the colors. The furniture design and placement did not align with me. It was not peaceful, and it just did not have that home feeling. One of my coworkers recommended this lady to me. I sold that ugly furniture and hired a reputable firm to come and design my place according to my taste and lifestyle." Victoria says, "Well, this is something that you would see in a high-end furniture showroom, it's beautiful. I would have never put burnt orange and gray together. Oh, I just love the modern oversized burnt orange chairs, especially next to the enormous window, and where did you find this white marble and gray coffee table? Especially in this size? This thing is huge." She runs her hands down the leather gray sectional sofa with attached chase and says, to Jamison, "Very nice!" She eyeballs the white pillows that accent the all-white stone end tables and sofa table. The large gray ottoman is sitting on the opposite side of the chase for extra seating. Meanwhile, Jamison is in the kitchen, cooking up a storm. Victoria is looking out at the city's beautiful skyline and becomes a little sad. She admires the caramel-colored wood ceiling with chrome recess lighting and a large white ceiling fan. "This place is magnificent," she says.

A two-sided fireplace encased in white and gray marble separates the living room and dining room. The white oak hardwood floors make the rooms look enormous. He has an oversized chrome floor lamp that just reaches the top of the ceiling before it bends over the sofa. The curtains are white linen flowing as the ceiling fan turns.

Jamison says, "Why do you look sad Victoria? Other than my cooking, what is the real reason you came over?" He hands her a glass of wine and she takes a seat at the dining room table. Jamison says, V, he is the only one who calls her that. "You look sad, and you know, I know you, so what is it?" Victoria says, "You ever have that feeling that things are about to drastically change but you don't know which direction or why?" Jamison replied, "Yes, I know exactly what you mean, but you have to be intentional, take control of the wheel and push the gas petal. Change will come, one way or another. You have to be prepared for it and know how to control it." Victoria smiles and says, "That's why I love talking to you Jamison, you have so much wisdom and you always know what to say. You are that sibling I longed to have growing up as an only child. I didn't fit in anywhere, and I didn't have any genuine friends. I'm so glad our paths crossed in college and that we are friends for life." Jamison had poured himself a whiskey neat while she was sitting at the table. He placed her plate of vegetable stir-fry with steak and mushrooms in front of her and poured two glasses of spring water into the water goblets.

Jamison put his glass in the air and says to Victoria, "A toast to best friends." He put on an island CD and turned the volume up as a statement of no more talking. Victoria is feeling so much better now. The liquid courage along with the melody of the music that is playing, she decides she would go to the casino after she leaves Jamison's place to win her money back. She offers to help Jamison clean up while hurrying out the door. Jamison says, "Just like I said, you only came over to eat." They laugh, Victoria replies, "And free advice from my best friend. It's always good to have quiet time with you, without the others. I will see you tomorrow morning." Jamison says, "Keep your eyes peeled" and gives her a wink as she exits his apartment.

He takes his whiskey neat and goes into his home office and sits at his desk. He is looking over some documents and his new robotic surgical design plans. He is thinking about what Victoria said about the feeling that things are about to change drastically. He is thinking about Dr. Naomi and Jon and their proposition. He then remembers the answer he gave Victoria, about taking the wheel and pushing the gas petal, taking control and being intentional. He decides at that moment he would join them. He just didn't want to tell them his decision yet, he wanted to make them stir a bit. He goes into his bedroom and takes a nap.

JADE

The Morning After

Jade went out on a run. She loves the trails in her neighborhood. The sun was shining oh so brightly. This is the perfect weather for a long run and a perfect way to prepare her mind for exiting the city tomorrow. While running, her mind imagines the warm sun and the white sandy beach front villa she will relax in for the next seven days. She can't wait to see the reaction on Lydia and Victoria's faces when they find out she signed them up for para sailing, mountain climbing, boat excursions and more. She lets out a laugh and continues her ten-mile run.

She heads home to her condo at four twenty East Waterside

Drive, her condominium is on the twelfth floor. She had it renovated prior to moving in. This condo has a large foyer that makes a statement upon entry. There is a large round walnut table that has a tall vase in the center. It is filled with a multicolored flower arrangement, that is tall enough to just about touch, the five-foot hanging chandelier. The condo has a split floor plan with natural colored hardwood floors throughout. The view overlooks the lake from the wrap around balcony, which she can access from her living room and the master bedroom. The large en-suite master bedroom has an enormous walk-in closet that is large enough to hold a full-size bed, dresser, and two nightstands. It has wall to wall shelving for all her shoes and accessories. One wall has built-in drawers and cabinetry. As you walk a little deeper into the closet, you walk into a huge open room; she even put a chandelier in the closet. This room has two yellow round leather armless chairs and floor to ceiling mirrors on each wall. She designed this area to use as a dressing room.

The master bedroom is spacious and vibrant, with a custom-made oversized king bed. The massive headboard is lavender velvet, with six big silver buttons in rows of four. The bed linens are white with lavender and yellow floral print. Her curtains are lavender and silver that cover the gigantic window. There is a very large purple shag rug that takes up most of the room, in one corner of the room sits a yellow oversized leather chair. The private balcony overlooks Lake Shore Drive.

The second bedroom has a queen-size bed, the color theme is tan and powder blue. It has a tropical feel to it. There is an oversized window that has a spectacular view of the city skyline. The guest bathroom has herringbone marble counter-tops, walnut cabinetry, and a large tile stand up shower encased in glass. There is a large claw-foot tub by the window. This bathroom has crystal light fixtures that match the others, through the condo. The color scheme is tan and powder blue to match the rest of the home's decor. Jade is constantly cleaning as this has become an obsession for her.

The spacious open kitchen has modern lacquered cabinetry and high-end appliances and a large walk-in pantry. The large island which separates the kitchen and the living room has a tan and black marble countertop with bar seating. The bar seats are armless and backless stainless-steel square shaped.

The living room has wall to wall windows with the city view. The sofa is tan with big buttons along the back, trimmed with silver beading along the edges, the matching loveseat faces the sofa. There is a huge oval-shaped walnut coffee table placed in the center and matching end tables. The room has several artificial trees in colorful flowerpots, the greenery warms the gigantic room. She accessorized the room with a large shag powder blue rug. The large windows are covered with powder blue and tan shears. Colorful abstract paintings are throughout the condo. The dining room has an enormous walnut table, that seats six. The high-back chairs have a grey and tan pattern, and there is an oversized tan and black rug under the table.

The den is her home office. No abstract here, just a wall full of degrees and certificates of accomplishment. Her law school diploma is oversized and centered on the wall as the focal point.

As she enters her building, she stops to check her mail before getting on the elevator since she didn't have time to do so yesterday. Oh, yesterday was a wash between a long day at the office and rushing to the SPOT for dinner; which turned into a much longer night than she had planned. As she sorts through the mail while getting on the elevator, she sees a letter from her sister, her heart sinks. The elevator reached the twelfth floor and as the doors open; she slowly walks to her condo with a sad look on her face. She enters the foyer and heads straight to her office and files the letter away, she never opened it. She decided she would deal with it when she returns from vacation. She says out loud, "All they ever do is lie and complain so why should I be in a hurry to read the letters." She heads for the shower to wash off the sweat and the hurt she is feeling now since seeing that letter.

She pulls out black riding pants and a burgundy long sleeve off the shoulder sweater. She puts on riding boots and adds a small beaded pearl necklace with pearl drop earrings. She adds a pearl ring and matching bracelet. She put on her channel number five perfume, adds a touch of makeup, lipstick and grabs her jacket. She's thinking, *I'm starving, that's why I don't like to go out drinking. I know I only had wine, but when I drink, I eat as if I smoked marijuana. I swear, alcohol gives me the munchies.*

Jade takes a drive out of the city to a quiet cafe she visits frequently. She takes her case files with her to do a couple hours of reading, then she needs to go home and finish packing for the early airport arrival. She heads to the underground garage where she parks her champagne twenty nineteen Lexus LX 570 SUV. She opens the sunroof and heads out of the city. She loves to feel the breeze in her hair, and on this cool fall day, she has her heat on blast because she has the sunroof open. Crazy right! She turns on the radio and listens to the Saturday afternoon old school remix. She nods her head to the beat for the thirty-minute ride.

She thought, turning the radio up would take her mind off the letter, but it didn't. Her mind wondered, what if something is wrong back home? Nah, they would have called instead of writing a letter. Jade's sister struggles with bipolar disorder and needs to stay on her meds to control it. So Jade is thinking, maybe she is having one of her episodes and wrote me a crazy letter again like she did a few months ago. The thirty-minute ride seems like an hour because her mind continues to take her back to her childhood, which wasn't so great. Her life looked good on the outside to the community she grew up in and her church, but her home life was total chaos. She never felt like she belonged. She had both parents in the home and two older siblings, much older than she. Her parents told her they had her while going through the change. Jade's parents made her feel like they did not want her. She had two older sisters, Janice, is fifteen years older and Jessica is seventeen years older. Jade pretty much grew up as an only child. Her parents never bonded with her, and Jade always felt like her parents put her off on her older siblings to care for her. Because of the lack of communication and love in the household, Jade became a loner and an introvert. She didn't have very many friends. Her parents were very strict on her and she could not have much of a social life; especially when she reached high school age. Jade just buried herself in her studies to take her mind off of her home life, or lack of. She suffered with depression as a child and believes her parents did as well. They allowed no discussions about this in the home. Everyone was always whispering and would hush when she entered the room. She could not tell if they were talking about her or her sister Janice, but they always had a serious look on their faces. Jade says out loud, "I don't think I've ever seen my parents smile, except for the day, I told them I was moving to Chicago for college. I think they threw the biggest party ever when I left." Jade still suffers with depression and running, and exercising helps her to deal with it.

She arrives at her favorite cafe, shook her head really hard, and tells herself, *shake it off Jade, it was just a letter. I will not let this spoil my vacation, I should be celebrating.* She grabs her leather bag out of her SUV and just as she hit the door locks on her key fob, a gentleman stops her and says, "Such a big car for a little lady." She gives him a look that should have sent him running, and replies, "Is that why you drive that big pickup truck?" She then turns her head swiftly and walk into the cafe. As she enters, she lets out a big smile from cheek to cheek because her favorite server is working today. Jade says, "Hey Susan, how are you?" Susan says with excitement, "Jade, where have you been? I missed you!" She motions Jade to her favorite quiet corner table, tucked away from the public. Jade says, "I have been working long hours and just couldn't get in here the last couple of weeks. In fact, I have work to review now and I'm starving." Susan asked, "Are you having your usual?" Jade says, "You know it!"

Jade looks at the Lake Front Hospital files to see all prior and current litigations. Susan brings over a hot tea and places it on the table. Jade was so busy reading; she didn't notice it. She skims and reads that Dr. Naomi Lee had a case that settled out of court and cost the hospital two point two million dollars in settlement. Jade says to herself; *I've heard that name before, I just can't put my finger on it and not in a case file or mediation.* Susan brings her food; she quickly closes the file and enjoys her entrée. After she finishes her meal and chats with Susan about her upcoming vacation. She opens another file to look over the open litigations. She reads about a few patients complaining of misdiagnosis. They will more than likely be thrown out of court because from the notes, the patient's symptoms warranted the diagnosis and procedure. Jade is so relieved that she doesn't have very many open cases to catch up on, it would ruin her vacation. She skimmed through a few closed case files and had a second cup of tea. She looked a little deeper at Dr. Naomi Lee's file; Jade is impressed that she is the chief of surgery and she is the number one transplant surgeons in the country. Jade smile and says, "Another one for the ladies!" She finishes her tea, leaves Susan a big tip, then heads back to the city to pack and get ready for her vacation. She now wishes she had used Jamison's services but at the same time she couldn't see paying money for something she could do herself.

CHAPTER FIVE

The Vacation

HERE WE GO

The Vacation

Victoria says, "Oh! I am soo sleepy," as she is thinking to herself, *I can't believe I stayed out until midnight last night. I've only had two hours of sleep, thanks to Jade with these early flights. I guess I will snore all the way to Atlanta, and I hope whoever is sitting next to me has earplugs. She showers and washes her hair to get rid of the smoke smell, to hide the evidence.* She then calls a Lift to take her to O'Hare airport. In the meantime, she calls Jade and Lydia to make sure they are on their way. Jade answers, "Girl, I'm already at the airport and Lydia is on her way." Victoria says, "Okay, I should arrive in the next thirty minutes.

She makes her way down to the lobby and the Lift driver loads her two oversized suitcases. While in the Lift, her mind drifts to last night. After she left Jamison's place, she went back to the casino, determined to win her money back or at least half of it. She used the five thousand dollars she transferred from her savings yesterday and went straight to the blackjack table. She lost two thousand dollars within the first hour. The loss devastated Victoria, so she went to the bar to have a stiff drink and to regroup. Her cell phone rings, the caller ID shows, unknown caller, she hesitates to answer, but just as she says "Hello," the caller hangs up. Victoria disregards the call. She needs to get her mind in a *Ready to win mode.* She went over to the slot machine, this time and immediately she hit a jackpot for ten thousand dollars. She was so excited, she about peed on herself. "Oh, My Goodness!" She yelped with excitement!

Victoria arrives at the airport; they board the aircraft and Victoria sleeps during the entire flight to Atlanta. Jamison asked Victoria why was she so tired? What did she do when she left his place? Victoria said, "I went home, but I just didn't sleep well last night, I was afraid I would oversleep and miss my flight." Once they boarded the plane for the last flight to St. Lucia, Victoria falls back to sleep. Actually, they all went to sleep.

They finally arrived in St. Lucia; they admired the golden sun glowing over the deep blue ocean while strolling through the airport to retrieve their luggage. They find the sign that says

Calabash Cove Resort and get in a taxi. On the way to the resort, the taxi driver is giving them a tour of the island.

The taxi driver said, "We are going past the Vicibou Caldera, it formed thirty-two thousand to thirty-nine thousand years ago." The driver proceeds to tell them about a few other major attractions, they should see while they are on the island, such as Marigot Bay, Sulphur Springs Park, the Diamond Botanical Garden, and the Waterfall mineral bath, just to name a few. Jade was quiet during the ride as she has already made a reservation for every attraction the taxi driver just mentioned plus, snorkeling, zip lining and hiking. She thought to herself; *They were not interested in hearing the entire agenda Friday night, so what I have lined up will surprise them.*

They arrive at the Calabash Cove Resort. They are amazed how beautifully it is nested on a hillside, sloping slightly, overlooking the Caribbean Sea, and has direct access to the beach. From this view, the sea almost looks turquoise and not as blue as it did from the airport. The beautiful gardens, tropical trees and vegetation give this place a calming, relaxing peacefulness to it. The Manor House is at the top of the hill and has lovely suites, a restaurant and pool, surrounded by luxurious suites and cottages that all face the ocean. As they get out of the taxi and gather their luggage, the luxurious beauty of the resort had them speechless. The staff came out to greet them and take their luggage to their respective suite. They were each greeted by a personal concierge to handle their needs individually. The check in was quick, the ladies had individual junior suites side by side, and Jamison had a cottage that wasn't too far away. They each agreed to get settled, shower, then meet for a late lunch in the Wind Song Restaurant at the top of the hillside.

They enter their rooms with their concierge, who opens the curtains for them and gives each of them a quick tour. The concierge also showed them the amenities in their suites. Goes over the special events and services, such as the Spa, bar, swim-up pool bar and remind them that this is an all-inclusive resort.

Lydia immediately calls Victoria and tells her to connect her with Jade. They each squeal and Lydia says, "Jade, the brochures did not do this place justice." Victoria says, "I've had luxury in my life, but this is extraordinary. Do you all have balconies off your living rooms?" Lydia and Jade say, "Yes, and the whirlpool tub is huge." They each asked for their suite numbers, and before unpacking and showering as planned, they run to each other's suite, to see the different color schemes of each one. They are now in Victoria's room and she opens a bottle of wine. They each grab a wine glass heads to the balcony and toast to being there together. As they overlook the beautiful ocean and beach, they polish off the entire bottle of wine and suddenly realized they had not unpacked or showered yet. Jade said, "Jamison is probably ready, and we probably should have waited for him to have this toast." Lydia says, "Relax Jade, Jamison is probably finishing a glass of whiskey by now and we will have the entire week to toast to each other." They giggle and head to their perspective suits and rush to get ready. They both hug and thank Jade again for the beautiful accommodations that exceeded their expectations.

VICTORIA

The Vacation

Victoria is thinking while she is showering. *Wow, I can't believe how beautiful and peaceful my suite is. They draped my canopied bed in long white shears. The linens are turquoise, gray and white, the pillows on the bed, sofa and chairs have the Piton mountains and hillside on them. Although, I'm exhausted from being at the casino way too late last night. I can't wait to explore the resort and attractions. Jade did a fantastic job with this trip, and now I feel bad for complaining about the early flight.* She unpacks all of her clothes so that when she returns tonight, she will not have to deal with it. She is so happy to have won her money back last night after a horrible week of losing. She got on her knees and thanked God for safe travels, for her friends, her career, and she promised to not put herself in that situation again by gambling. She is grateful for God's blessings.

She receives a text message from Jade, it reads, *are you ready? Lydia and I are on our way to get you, then to the dining room to meet Jamison. He is already there. Jade replies, yes, grabbing my shoes and heading out the door. Will meet you at the entrance.* They complement each other's outfits; these ladies know how to make a fashion statement. They arrive at the Windsong Restaurant, which has seating outdoors on the covered deck that overlooks the pool and ocean. It is still early in the evening, so the sun is shining brightly and there are no clouds in the sky. White tablecloths elegantly cover the tables. The plate settings are bright and colorful with a tropical theme. As they take their seat at the table, Jamison says, "Have whatever you like Ladies, it's on me!" With a big smile. They laugh! Lydia says, "Why thank you very much Jamison, what would we do without you?" The server comes over right away to greet them and ask for their drink orders. The server also says to them, "This is an all-inclusive resort, so it's all you can eat and all you can drink. If you order something that you dislike, feel free to send it back and try another dish." They each look at Jamison and place their drink orders. Victoria says, "I will have an apple martini, please." Lydia says, "I will have a cosmopolitan martini, please." Jade says, "I will have a glass of Chardonnay, thank you." Jamison orders a whiskey neat.

Jade looks at Lydia and says, "Speaking of whiskey neat, don't you want to change your order Lydia?" they laugh in a loud belly laugh. Jamison says, "Hurry and look at the menu, I'm ready to order. I have already looked at it and know what I want. Since you ladies took so long to shower and get dressed. I had time to tour the place, have a drink at the bar and check out the menu." The ladies laugh as they grab their menus, thinking about how they were having a glass of wine on Victoria's balcony and that is really what took them so long. The server comes back with their drinks and takes their order. Jamison says, "I will have the St. Lucian red snapper filet." Victoria and Jade orders the same. They look at Lydia because there are few vegetarian options. Lydia says, "I will have the caramelized plum and soursop duck breast but hold the duck." The server looked puzzled, she exclaimed, "I'm a vegetarian so I would like for the cook to not put the duck or any meat on my plate please." The server says, "Oh, okay! No problem, would you like extra vegetables or soup instead?" Lydia says, "Extra vegetables would be great please."

After the server leaves the table, they look at each other with misty eyes, and Jamison says, "Let's have a toast Ladies." He always referred to them as Ladies when they were all together. Jamison is a very respectful gentleman. They each raise their glass and Jamison says, "To us, we are a long way from the little scared college freshmen we were twelve years ago. Look at us now, let's toast to everlasting friendship." They take a sip and smile at each other. Jamison says, "These days, it is hard to find friendship as solid as ours." Jade says, "It's because we are true to ourselves and each other. We do not keep any secrets from each other. We have a relationship where we can tell each other anything. We have such a powerful bond." Victoria says, "I'm proud to call you my friends, each of you are a friend that is closer than any brother." Jade says, "I am my brother's keeper!" They all repeat after Jade with their glasses held high and toast again with laughter.

The server brings out the food and everything looks amazing. The food was spectacular, and the setting was something you could only dream about. They order another round of drinks. This time Lydia replied, "These are on me!" They laugh. After this round of drinks, they go out on the patio and relax on the beach in the recliner chairs. They talk about how they first met. Lydia and Jamison were in an algebra class together their first semester, and this is where their friendship started. Jamison looks over at Lydia and says, "Yes, I was in algebra and this mean skinny girl comes in the classroom with her nose turned up as if the room was disgusting. She looked around for a seat that wasn't next to anyone else and sat down." Jade laughs and retorts, "That is a lie, I did not have my nose turned up!" Lydia says, "I can see that, I had a similar experience when I met her." Jade says, "I was not a snob!" Victoria laughs and says "Well, you kind of still are, but you have earned it being a big-time corporate lawyer and all." Jamison says, "Oh, we have to congratulate Jade on her new big account." Victoria and Lydia smile, and Lydia says, "What new account?"

Jade smiles and tells them, "I am now the legal representation for Lake Front Memorial hospital. They dropped the promotion in my lap on Friday, and I was told to be up to date on the case files when I returned to work next week. I'm not sure if this is a blessing or a curse because of the timing." Victoria and Lydia let out a yelp and says, "Congratulations honey! This is huge and this could be big for your career." Lydia smiles and says, "I'm so happy for you and you deserve it. You have worked your butt off for that firm and they should have made you a partner a long time ago." Victoria says, "I know we have rules to not bring work on vacation, but this is different." Victoria says, "Do what you need to do but just try to relax and have fun." Lydia and Jamison shake their heads in agreement.

It relieved Jade that they took the news so well. Then Jade says, "Well, I'm not looking at any work tonight, that's for sure. Tonight, is all about us. Oh, and by the way Jamison, I don't appreciate you calling me a skinny snob." Jamison laughs and says, "You say that every time I tell that story of how we met. It took her two weeks to even speak to me." Jade laughs and says, "I was shy and didn't know anyone, so I was playing the tough girl role." Victoria says, "I met Jade in the school cafeteria, it was probably our first week of school and she was sitting at a table all by herself. I thought she was from the city because she looked so mean, but me being the friendly chatter box I am, I went over to her table and said, is anybody sitting here?" Jade looked up at me and smiled and said, no, no one is sitting here, and you are welcome to join me." That was the start of our friendship. We didn't have any classes together that semester, but we exchanged numbers." Lydia chimes in and says, "I met Jamison in anatomy and physiology class our freshman year. We became study partners because we also had the same biology class together. He introduced me to Jade, and Jade introduced me to Victoria." Jamison holds up his glass and says, "To Jade, the connect." They all laugh.

The server comes over to ask if they would like another round of drinks. They each nod their heads yes. Jade asks Lydia, "Now don't you want a whiskey neat?" They laugh. Lydia says, "I don't think so, I will just stick with my cosmopolitan martini's or wine, thank you very much." She tells them about how she thought she had died when she opened her eyes yesterday morning and how she found some dude's number written on a napkin from the SPOT. Jamison said, "I left you at the bar with one of your coworkers, you said you were okay and that you would take an Uber home." Lydia said, "Yes, I did, but for the life of me, I don't remember meeting this guy." Victoria asked, "Did you call him?" Lydia replied, "No," and sips her drink. Jade says, "Well I don't blame you; you can't trust your judgment after drinking as many whiskeys as you had." They blurt out in laughter. Victoria says, "Do you think you would recognize him if you see him again?"

Lydia replies, "Probably not because I can't remember how his number got in my purse."

The server comes back with their drinks and asked if anyone wanted desert? They each replied, "Not at this time, but I'm sure I will want something later." Victoria asked Jade, "What was your crazy roommate's name again our freshman year." Jade about chokes on her drink and says, "Crazy Stacy? The roommate of the year? Yea, she was a psycho case. It took me an entire year to realize she was on drugs. I must have been young and naïve back then to not know she was on drugs." Victoria retorted, "We all were young and naïve back then."

LYDIA

The Vacation

Lydia says, "Let's take a walk around this gorgeous resort, I'm sure we can take our drinks with us and I want to see this cottage Jamison is staying in. He had to be special and not get a junior suite like the rest of us." Victoria and Jade said, "let's stop by his cottage on our tour of the resort." Jamison says, "No problem, you Ladies could have gotten cottages, but I thought it was safer for you to be in the junior suite than secluded in a cottage all alone. That's why I made the recommendations for you three to get a junior suite." The ladies, each say in unison, "Ahh, Okay," as they node their heads. Lydia says, "That's why you are the MAN

Jamison, you always look out for us and we are lucky to have you as our friend. As they walk along the gardens with beautiful walkways, Lydia closes her eyes and inhales with a deep breath to smell the exotic flowers, luscious plants and breathtaking trees in the gardens. She can hear the sounds of the hummingbirds and wind chimes. She can feel the warm breeze upon her face and feel it as it blows through her long dark hair. In this moment, Lydia imagines being all alone and has tuned out the chatter from the others, as they experience the splendor of this resort. She snaps back into reality as she hears Victoria say, "Oh, I see the Spa, I want to go inside to book a massage and facial for tomorrow morning. Come on, let's go inside and make appointments for tomorrow."

The lounge area has five caramel colored wicker chairs with cream colored cushions. The chairs are seated in a half circle facing the ocean. The flooring is large rock petals surrounded by a beautiful flower garden. They each take a seat to rest from the walk and just enjoy the breathtaking view in silence. Finally, Lydia says, "Look, you can get a massage outside on the outer deck that has a view of the ocean." They pick up a brochure she was referring to. It says the spa offers a wide range of treatments that combine European technique with St. Lucia's tradition of using plant and food-based curatives. We design each treatment to cleanse the body of stress, rejuvenate the spirit and relax the mind. The exfoliation products are all organic and made from local products. Our therapists will be happy to show the different benefits between a coffee or papaya scrub, and more. Guest always has a choice in the preferred location of their massage. Whether on the boardwalk, the gazebo or the privacy of their room patio or cottage living room. They walk towards the entrance to get more information.

Lydia says to the receptionist, "I will have the Island Fruit body scrub, and a fifty-minute deep tissue massage, and the intensive spa facial. I would like to have it out on the gazebo tomorrow. What times do you have available?" The receptionist asks, "Would you all like to come at the same time?" Jade says, "I will take the same time she has." Victoria says, "Yes, I would like to come at the same time as well, if possible." Jamison says, "I will call in the morning to schedule a time." The receptionist says, "I can get all three of you in tomorrow at ten o'clock, will this work for you?" Lydia says, "Perfect!" The receptionist looks at Victoria and says, "Would you like the gazebo or one of our private spa rooms?" Victoria requested a private spa room with peace and quietness, as she orders the same therapeutic treatment as Lydia. Jade asked, "I will also take a private spa room and I would also like the sixty-minute intensive spa facial and the fifty-minute seaweed body wrap." The receptionist says, "Okay ladies, I have you down for ten and we will see you in the morning." As they exit the spa, Jade looks at Lydia and says, "Yes, you need a deep tissue massage and island fruit body scrub to detox all of that whiskey out of your body from Friday night." They laugh, but Lydia is thinking to herself. *If they only knew about the night Sam and I had last night, they would realize I need more than detox.*

The sun is starting to set, so they went up to the C Bar to watch the sunset and listen to some live music; and of course; have more drinks. The C Bar offers stunning views of the sea from the comfort of the beautiful couches, lounging areas or intimate tables. The C Bar also looks out over the infinity pool and their table overlooked the ocean. They order appetizers and more drinks. Lydia has switched to a glass of Merlot instead of a cosmopolitan. Jade snickered at her and says, "No more cosmos's? What?" Lydia ignores her remark and faces the ocean. She is taking in the setting. She has worked very hard her entire life; she is finally in a relaxed place and life is good. This is the first time in many years, she has not had to worry about her sister's health or her parent's lack of finances.

The drinks and appetizers come to the table, they nibble and sip in silence, as they watch the sunset over the ocean. The band is playing island music and Lydia is thinking, *I could not have imagined the St. Lucia experience being this great.* Lydia says, "Can we just stay here forever?" They each sigh and Victoria says, "Yes we can, remember, Jamison is paying the bill." They each laugh and bob their heads to the music. Lydia is thinking about all that she has accomplished and overcome from her past and how great things are now. She is reminiscing about her decision to meet Sam for dinner last night. They had such a wonderful conversation and such a good time together. They ended up going out dancing, something she has not done in years. Sam was a perfect gentleman. He is a surgeon at Stonehedge Memorial Hospital, in Evanston, Illinois. They have so much in common. He also worked in ER for years and went to the same medical school as she did, but many years earlier. Sam is ten years older and Lydia admired his wisdom and experience. They shared many ER stories over dinner, some they could laugh about and some they were very passionate about. Sam also really loved his patients and loves what he does. He too is vegetarian, which was surprising to Lydia. He is also a wonderful dancer and jokester. She really enjoyed his company and for the life of her, she still did not remember meeting him Friday at the SPOT and still did not remember exchanging phone numbers.

Jamison breaks the silence and says, "Lydia, you remember our biology professor, Mr. Neilson?" Lydia laughs and says, "Yes, he didn't seem to know how to match his clothing. The man would wear stripe shirts with plaid pants. We used to call him Mr. Polyester. His wardrobe seemed stuck in the seventies." Jamison and the rest of them burst out laughing. Victoria says, "I remember you all talking about him when we were in college." Jamison said, "He may have had a wardrobe from the seventies, but the man was a genius. He could explain the most complicated text, to where an elementary school child understands. He truly had the gift to teach." Lydia says, "What makes you bring him up

Jamison?" Jamison replied, "I read his obituary in the newspaper last week and wasn't sure if you knew he had passed away." Lydia said, "No, I did not know about his passing, how sad. I'm so happy I was one of his students." Jamison said, "Yes, same here; the man had so much wisdom, not just about the human body but also about life. I really admired him, and I too am so happy to have been a part of his legacy. Did you know he was an organ donor? He also donated his body to research." Lydia says, "Wow, I would have never pictured him as a donor, but I'm happy to know that he was. He will help so many lives by donating his organs." She tells them about her little sister being a recipient of a heart transplant. That is why she wanted to become a doctor and surgeon. They each looked at her with compassion because she has never shared this.

Jade asked, "How old was she? I didn't know you had a little sister." Lydia says, "She was eight years old, and I was fourteen when she received the heart transplant. She was born with abnormal heart valves, and when she was a baby, we were living in Portugal at the time. She caught in infection, rheumatic fever, and developed endocarditis. Therefore, we came to America, so she could get the best medical help possible. She was in and out of hospitals most of her life because of her illness. As she got older, her condition worsened, and they placed her on the donor list."

Jamison leans in as if Lydia was whispering, he asked, "How long was she on the donor list before receiving the transplant?"

She replied, "Five years, and countless hospital stays and ER visits. But thank God for a donor." Jade asked, "How is she doing now?" Lydia replies, "She still has difficulties, it's been fifteen years since her transplant. She is on anti-rejection medications, she will have to take for the rest of her life, but overall, she is doing well." Jamison says, "Wow Lydia, I never knew that. My mom was on the donor list for seven years when she died from kidney failure. I was a junior in high school, so I also believe in the organ donor program and process." Jade says, "We have known each other for twelve years and I never knew this about either of you." Victoria says, "I'm so sorry both of you had to experience this, I also did not know." Lydia looks at Jamison and says, "Jamison and I'm sorry about your mother." Then she says, enough of this sad talk, "Let's all get up and dance, to love, life and each other!" They all gather in a circle in front of the band, holding hands, dancing like they had never danced before.

JAMISON

The Vacation

Jamison wakes up in his beautifully decorated cottage with quite the hangover. This is not typical of him as he was never a big drinker. In fact, neither of them was big drinkers, smokers or used any substances. They are each very health conscious and are very career focused. But lately, they are all drinking a little excessively. Speaking of career, Jamison's cell phone rings and it's Dr. Naomi Lee. Jamison answers, "Good morning Doc. How are you?" She says, "I Just finished another surgical procedure with your surgical instrument, it was very successful. Your tool cut my surgical time in half. It is not only valuable for us surgeons to get more surgeries done in a day, but it is also beneficial for the patience because they are not under anesthesia as long." Jamison says, "Yes, we have already made that determination, so what's on your mind?" Jamison is not one for small talk and it is very difficult to fool him. Dr. Naomi finally says, "I hear you didn't give us a solid answer on Friday afternoon. Did you make your decision yet?" Jamison lets out a long sigh and said with a big smile on his face, "Yes, Doc, I'm in." She could feel his smile through the phone. She exclaimed with excitement, "Good Jamison, this is very good. Welcome to another world." She says to Jamison, "Enjoy your vacation because you will be busy when you return to the city. We will spend a lot of time together." Jamison says, "Will do, keep your eyes peeled."

He hangs up. Jamison is feeling relieved he finally gave them an answer and suddenly realizes life will never be the same. He calls the spa and makes an appointment for nine o'clock. He wanted to get there before the ladies. He also asked for a private room for his deep tissue massage and sixty-minute facial. He jumps in the shower and orders room service. He wanted a little time alone, to think about his life as it is now because it is about to change. Jamison is also thinking heavily about his mother this morning, he has never shared her death with anyone before last night. He can't believe, he and Lydia have a similar family history and never discussed it with each other. He felt a connection to her when they first met (spiritually) but he didn't understand it. Except for their similar interest in the human anatomy and the several different languages they both spoke. They would often speak to each other in unique languages to tick Victoria and Jade off on purpose. It was the one thing they shared that they didn't share with the others.

Jamison ordered a local newspaper. He is aware we are in the digital world, but he is a little old fashion with his news. He likes the smell and feel of good old newspaper. He reads the local news while eating a light breakfast and takes three Tylenol for his massive headache. He is now, thinking about how he will need to cut back on the alcohol. This all you can eat and all you can drink can get him in trouble. He really needs to keep his eyes peeled and develop a strategy for his alternative lifestyle. He is happy about his decision, smiles and heads to the Spa.

It is one o'clock Monday afternoon and they meet up for lunch at the Windsong restaurant to discuss the plans for the rest of the week. They sit outside along the outer edge at a table overlooking the pool and ocean. Victoria is wearing an enormous hat as if she were on the beach, she looks like she is a undercover movie star as she walks to the table with a swag. Jamison and Jade look at each other and laugh. Lydia says, "She is so dramatic, but we gotta love her."

The server comes to the table and says, "Whiskey neat and wine for the Ladies?" They each blurt out in unison, "No, water please!" Lydia retorts, "With lemon on the side in a separate bowl on ice, please." They quickly look over the lunch menu so they will be ready to order when the server returns. Jade says, "Well, I have a sailboat tour scheduled for five o'clock this evening. It will be perfect for your hat, Victoria." They laugh. Victoria changes the subject and asked, "How was your spa treatment this morning? Mine was fabulous." Lydia said, "I can tell by your swagger when you walked to the table." They each laugh again. Jade says, "It was the best experience ever. I forgot how good it feels to get a body wrap and relax. My skin feels like silk and I feel so rejuvenated. I'm glad I started my day with three Tylenol and a big breakfast." Lydia said, "I thought I was taking excellent care of myself by exercising and eating right, but the massage and facial is an experience like no other. I will make sure I treat myself to both more often when I get back to the city. I hear other doctors talk about going to the spa, but I looked at them as being snooty and boogie. But not anymore, everyone should treat themselves to this experience at least once a quarter." Jamison says, "Mine was spectacular.

The server brings their food and they eat in silence for the first time, and neither of them notices. They each have heavy thoughts on their minds and the detoxing spa treatment stirred up a few emotions, so they are in a different space right now. The server comes over to refresh their glasses of water and ask if they are ready for an adult beverage yet. They each say, "No thank you, we will just have water." Jamison says, "How did everyone sleep last night? Did you Ladies feel safe?" They each said yes and stated how comfortable their beds were. Lydia asks Jamison how did his oversized king bed sleep? He replied, "It was a magnificent sleep." Victoria said, "I've never heard of a magnificent sleep," laughter. Jamison said, "That's the only description I could come up with. I had way too much alcohol last night, but I have to find out what kind of mattress is on the bed because I want to have one shipped to me." Jade said, "It is now three o'clock and we need to be downstairs at the entrance at four thirty for our ride to the ocean." Jamison tells Jade to bring the wine glasses and he will bring the wine for the sailboat ride. They each go back to their suites to prepare for the evening.

Jamison has a burst of excitement, as if he had received a new toy. He didn't understand this new feeling, but he had to contribute it to his new venture he was about to endure. On his way to his cottage, he spotted a beautiful female staring at him. She nods her head, and he nods back as he passes her and flashes those perfect white teeth. She was stunning and was with another female, so he figured she was not accompanied by a man. Jamison told himself to keep walking and not look back. He did just that. He did not look back but went to his cottage to get ready for the evening.

While relaxing in his cottage, his cell phone rings, he answers, "Hello!" The caller said, "Jamison, it's your father. How are you doing son." Jamison says, "Dad, I'm good, how are you? Is everything okay?" His father replies, "Yes, it is son, I was just thinking about you and wanted to call you. How is work going?" Jamison replies, "It's going great, I just designed a new surgical instrument that was very successful in a surgical procedure. I have a patent for it, and Lake Front Memorial Hospital is my first big client." Jamison's dad exclaimed, "Son, I knew you would be a successful engineer. You were always creative and passionate about fixing things to make them better; especially all of my electronics in the house. Boy, I used to come home and find you in your room with the television torn apart, because you wanted to figure out how it was put together. You used to drive me and your mother crazy with taking everything apart. Looks like all of that frustration paid off." Jamison replies, "Yes it did, I have another instrument I'm working on, it is currently in the lab."

His father says, "You are in St. Lucia, aren't you?" Jamison says, "Yes sir, we arrived yesterday." His father asked, "With Jade, Victoria, and Lydia?" Jamison says, "Yes, it's our annual vacation time." His dad says, "Son, when are you going to settle down and get married? I'm getting up in age and I would like to have some grandchildren before I get too old to enjoy them. Your brother is still missing, or should I say, he doesn't want to be found. So I guess it will be you to give me grandkids." Jamison pours a drink, something he had not planned to do today, but when his father starts this conversation, he needs a drink to remain calm. Jamison tells his father, "Dad, I'm in my prime, and my career is excelling. I will meet someone, get married someday and have lots of children for you, but this is not the right time." His father says, "I understand son, things are not the way they used to be. When your mother and I was growing up. Back in the day, you met a girl and married her. By the time you were twenty years old, you had at least one child, if not two. I know times are different now, but don't wait too long." His father laughs. Jamison said, "I won't make you wait too long dad, but right now I'm getting ready to go sailing with the ladies and I don't want to be late meeting up with them. Give mom my love (stepmom) and I will talk to you when I get back to the city." Jamison's dad ends the call with, "Keep your eyes peeled, son."

JADE

The Vacation

I'm so glad everyone enjoyed the sailboat tour of the island yesterday. Today we are touring Castries, which is the capital city centered on a harbor, that has the crater of an extinct volcano. It is also the port of call for major cruise lines and the Vigie Beach. The market yesterday, was a wonderful experience, to see and taste the exotic fruits and homemade banana rum sauce on the deserts. Victoria and Lydia went on a shopping excursion, and Jamison and I ate as much as they shopped. It surprised me they were willing to go kayaking along Rodney Bay to tour Pigeon Island. We swam, snorkeled and even went hiking. We had dinner at the

Beacon restaurant for an authentic cuisine experience; which had incredible panoramic views of the Pitons, and the food was amazing.

Wednesday, we toured the Pitons, the two volcanic formations that rise over the Caribbean Sea, and they are also the most iconic landmarks of St. Lucia. Victoria gave the tour guide a hard time because it took nearly three hours to climb one Gros Piton. We were like; you see how tall this mountain is so why wouldn't it take at least two hours to reach the top. We were surprised glamour girl agreed to climb it in the first place, so we expected her to complain. Once we climbed the *Stairway To Heaven*, and reached the top, the view was amazing. After seeing the Pitons from this level, Victorian apologized for complaining. We just laughed at her and I told her I knew she would appreciate it once she arrived at the top.

Thursday, we spent the day at the *Torallie Waterfalls*. It is a breathtaking waterfall that gushes fifty feet over the side of a cliff and cascades into a pool at the center of a beautiful landscaped garden. We walked across the bridges and walkways that lead us through the lush greenery and dazzling colors of this tropical paradise. Lucky for us, the force of the water was not too strong, so we stood under the waterfall for what seems like hours. It felt like we were getting shoulder and back massages from nature. We can now cross this off our bucket list along with hiking the Pitons.

We spent Thursday evening at our resort for dinner. We had an exciting and exhausting week and we only had two days left. After dinner, we went to our suites to retire early for the evening; since we had a full day on Friday, more tours, early morning zip-lining, massages and facials scheduled for the afternoon. We were flying back to the city Sunday morning, so we needed Saturday to rest and unwind. I also had some work to catch up on and needed to dig more into my case files.

Jade is sitting at the desk in her junior suite, she pulls out her iPad and case files while having a glass of wine. Although she had skimmed through them at the cafe last Saturday, she did not go through the closed files. She comes across another lawsuit, filed two years ago by a patient who claimed misdiagnosis, which resulted in losing a kidney. The discovery stated, the claimant underwent the procedure to have his left kidney removed at the recommendation of Dr. Naomi Lee, for a tumor on the kidney. The medical records state, the aggressive tumor would grow larger and the cancer could spread to other organs and into his lymph nodes. After having the kidney removed, the patient went through chemotherapy and radiation. At the end of the chemo sessions; he was miraculously cancer free. The case was closed because of lack of evidence of any wrongdoing. The lab results and radiology films showed a mass at the time of diagnosis.

Jade is now thinking about the prior cases she reviewed, and the same doctor's name continues to come up. After further research on this Dr. Naomi Lee, Jade remembers that she is the top transplant and cancer doctor in the United States. A document in the file from the hospital administrator, states, out of thousands of successful transplants and early detection, treatment of tumors and cancerous cells; she has saved, prolonged or provided a better quality of life for ninety-four percent of her patients. Although Jade had legal documentation that proved Dr. Naomi Lee did no wrongdoing; she had an uneasy feeling deep down in her gut about this doctor and the reputation of Lake Front Memorial.

She falls asleep with the case files and iPad in her lap. She dreamed about her childhood and her family. How she never fit in and always felt like an outcast. She dreamed about her sister's mental illness. The dream revealed to her, the mental illness was inherited from her father. He was a stern man, and it was nearly impossible to please him. How he whipped her with an extension cord because she left a dirty glass in the sink. He always found fault in everything she did. There were times, when he couldn't find anything wrong, but he still whipped her and would say to her; I'm sure you will screw up something before the week is out. Either way, this whipping is what you need. Jade's mother did nothing to help her, she was afraid of her dad and agreed with everything he said. She never gave her opinion or tried to rescue her from his abuse. The only person who would come to her rescue was her aunt Jessica. She was the oldest of the three girls, and she wasn't afraid to stand up to their parents.

Jade suddenly wakes up after the beating, panting heavily. She immediately looked at her legs and arms, fearing the scars were there. The dream was so real, she could feel the sting from the extension cord as if it were happening now. She's thinking; *I think that's why Janice suffers with bipolar disorder.* Now she feels guilty for not answering the unknown caller last Saturday, and for not opening the letter. But she just couldn't let that negative energy affect her vacation.

She pours herself another glass of wine to calm down. She has tried her best to put her childhood behind her and to communicate with them as little as possible. When Lydia, Victoria and Jamison go home for the holidays, Jade secretly travels to Los Angeles, California or Charlotte, North Carolina and pretends she is with her family. In fact, she hasn't been home to Seattle, Washington in eight years. She only went back home then to attend her nephew's high school graduation.

Jade is very fond of her nephew, Nicholas, and they have a powerful bond. He was the only person who understood the hell she was living through. Her sister Janice and Jessica had their own homes, so they were not there to see what she had to live with. Nicholas saw it when he came to visit his grandparents, which was often because his mother Janice would have her mental episodes, he would have to come live with them for a while. Jade remembers Nicholas telling her, one day auntie, we will get you out of here and I hope you never come back to these evil people. That is exactly what Jade did.

115

She falls back asleep and dreams again. This time, her dream is about the time during her senior year of high school when she walked in on her parents discussing the fact that they never wanted her, and how they got stuck raising her. She heard them say Janice was self-medicating with street drugs instead of taking her prescribed medication. Which resulted in Jade having a bipolar mother and crackhead father. It devastated Jade as she listened to their conversation in secret. For the first time in her entire life, she had an explanation for why her parents mistreated her and for all those years of anger towards her. For the first time, she felt relieved that she was not having a mental breakdown, and that she was not imagining being treated so badly by her parents, or should we say grandparents. Her sister Janice is actually her mother, and her nephew Nicholas was actually her brother. Jade wakes up again, this time in anger because of all the lies and deception. No child should ever have to endure such pain. She said, "They should have just given me up for adoption if they were going to treat me like hell."

She gets out of bed, and this time she opens a bottle of water. She had some cheese and crackers in the fridge, so she sat on the sofa, ate her snacks and watched the early morning news. She decided, no need to fall back to sleep and let her past continue to disturb her. So much for not bringing negative energy with her on vacation. After the news went off, she flipped through the channels and stopped on the channel of a minister preaching about forgiveness. Normally she would click right past it, but this time she tuned in and listen to the sermon. The minister said, *"You will not have any peace in your life until you deal with your past and forgive those who have hurt you. It is not your job to judge or punish them who harmed you. That's God's job. He has commanded us to love those who have harmed us, and we must forgive."* Jade feels a tear fall down her right cheek. She can't forgive them for abusing her and lying to her all her life. All this time, Nicholas was her brother, and she missed out on years of having a brother. The worst thing of it all is poor Nicholas doesn't even know. As soon as she overheard that conversation, she applied for colleges as far away from Seattle as possible. She is thinking, *I should have moved to Miami, Florida, but Northwestern University sent me an acceptance letter first, and I took the first offer letter to get me the heck out of Seattle.*

Jade falls asleep on the sofa and this time, she doesn't dream at all but gets about three hours of good sleep for the first time tonight.

CHAPTER SIX

My New Reality

VICTORIA

My New Reality

It's Sunday evening and they are back in the city. Victoria says to everyone as they are waiting for their luggage at baggage claim. "Wow, I'm so glad I had Saturday at the resort to just relax and catch up on some much-needed rest. This was the by far the best vacation I have ever had. Jade, you really outdid yourself this time! I admit, I was not happy about the hike or the zip-line adventure, but once I did it, I was so happy that I did. You really made me step out of my comfort zone and expand my horizon." She gives Jade a long, gentle hug. They all hug each other and agree with Jade.

Jamison says to Jade, "Now do you think either of us can top this vacation planning? Humm, you are going to have to continue to be our vacation planner. We can book flights or something like that, but what you laid out for us this time, was amazing and we love you for it."

Lydia says, "You know my planning skills are not good unless it involves shopping or surgery. Like Jamison said, we really need for you to remain as our vacation planner. I don't mind helping, but no one can top this one." Jade feels guilty for complaining about being the vacation planner. She is very happy, her best friends enjoyed everything she had planned. She smiles and tells them; she would carry on the tradition next year. Jamison says, "See you all at the SPOT Friday night around six thirty for dinner." They all agree and got into separate Ubers to go home.

As soon as Victoria arrives at her condo, she checks her mail and heads into her place. Although she loved the junior suite she stayed in last week, she missed her spacious, lovely condo. She is thrilled to be back in the city. As much as she would have loved to bring the tropical weather with her, she is glad to be home. She did not unpack; she decided she would use Jamison's service to unpack, take care of her laundry and dry cleaning drop off. Instead, she took a shower, changed clothes and went to her favorite place, the casino. She was truly having withdrawals from hearing the machines sing and the chatter from the card tables and billiards. She was like a junkie needing a fix. She pulls out her 2019 black Mercedes-Benz GLS Class SUV. This is her baby, black on black with black tinted windows. She chose this vehicle conceal her identity, being a bank president and all.

Upon arrival at the casino, she had a perplex feeling deep in her gut; not the feeling of she shouldn't be there, but a feeling like something big was about to happen. She couldn't put her finger on it but it wasn't excitement, it wasn't a warning; it wasn't sadness. It was something she could not describe. She went to the slot machines first to hear them sing to her ears. After about twenty minutes, she won close to two thousand dollars, and she was ahead. So she goes to her first love. And that is the blackjack table. Victoria figures, since she was up by two thousand dollars, what was the harm? She was doing very well tonight; she would win a hand, lose a hand, but lost nothing significant.

She went to a distinct part of the casino to try her luck at a different table. Once she sat down, she had that perplex feeling again. She won the first hand, and as the dealer was dealing the cards, she felt a presence around her. She quickly turned her head to look around and a gentleman passed by that resembled her ex-boyfriend from high school. She shakes it off and said says to herself, *couldn't be? But I have not seen him in twelve years, and why would he be in Chicago? Especially all the way from San Mateo California?* Victoria tries to find this gentleman again, but he disappeared in the crowd. It was getting late, and she needed to get to the bank early tomorrow to catch up on everything. This was the first time she had ever gone on vacation and did not check on the bank or her staff. This was truly an amazing vacation, and she was happy to go home, to her bed for the first time in a week.

Upon entering her condo, her cell phone rang; it was that unknown caller again; she let it ring a few times and then answered. The mysterious deep voice on the other end said, "Hello Victoria." Victoria said; "Who's calling and how did you get this number?" The caller was silent, Victoria had that perplexed feeling in her gut again. Then the caller said, "It's been a long time. It's good to hear your voice again." Her heart sank, she was silent. The caller said, "Hello, are you still there?" Finally, Victoria said, "Yes, I'm still here, and you still did not give me your name." The caller said, "I believe you already know who this is, but I will just tell you. It's me, Calvin, the man you left back home in California and didn't bother to look back."

Victoria's heart dropped to the floor; she couldn't say anything. So many mixed emotions flooded her heart and soul. She was literally shaking, and she couldn't speak. Calvin said, "What's the matter? Did you think our paths would never cross again? I know that's what you hoped for, but here we are." Victoria said, "Calvin, is it really you?" This time he was silent. She said, "You are right, I didn't think I would ever see you again." He blurted. "And if your parents had their way, we wouldn't be talking on the phone now." Victoria asked, "How did you find me and how did you get my phone number? It's private." Calvin said, "You know Victoria, I had no plans of ever speaking to you again. I never intended to be having this conversation with you, ever! Don't get it twisted because I was not looking for you at all. Circumstances, just happened to connect us together." Victoria asked, "What circumstances? What do you mean connect us together?" Calvin replied, "None of that matters now, what matters is that for the first time in twelve years, I have your attention without mommy and daddy's interference." Victoria was silent, then she said, "Calvin, you know I did not have a choice, we were young, and I did not have the confidence to stand up to my parents." Calvin said, "You mean you were a coward, right?" Victoria whispered, "Yes, I was a coward. I grew up accepting the cards they dealt me. I questioned nothing, especially my parents. You know the power they have in San Mateo. You would think they own the town." Calvin said, "You could have stood up to them, I was so angry with you, especially when they sent me to jail." Victoria said, "Calvin, I told them the sex was consensual. They knew that we were in love, they did this to punish us, me! And to this day, I still hate them for it. You know they hated me as much as they hated you. How could their trophy girl that they never wanted in the first place, end up pregnant by a boy from the other side of the tracks?" Victoria is crying, because all the hurt from her past is stirring up her emotions. Calvin said, "V, I know you were a scared little girl and didn't have a choice in having the abortion. You were only seventeen, but you turned your back on me." No one has ever called Victoria V, except Calvin and now Jamison. She forms a smile on her face and says softly, "Calvin, I never turned my back on you. My dad said he would have you killed if I ever spoke to you again. Those evil parents of mine had me on lock down, they even put a tracker on my car and cell phone. They changed my cell phone number and threaten to send me out of the country if I ever mentioned your name again."

Calvin said, "Your dad sent a couple of thugs to beat me up. A few days later, I was heading to work, and I was pulled over by a police officer. They searched my car and coincidently found a significant amount of cocaine under the driver seat. It mysteriously appeared there. They arrested me and I served ten years for a crime I did not commit. You know, I wasn't from the rich neighborhood you were from and my family didn't belong to any country clubs, but they were hardworking, honest people." He then yells, "I did not deserve to be framed and have my life taken from me."

Victoria is speechless. She was shaking again. She said, "Oh my God Calvin, I had no idea! As soon as I turned eighteen, I applied for college as far away as I could get, and I have never returned. My parents were so cruel, they told me they should have aborted me like they made me abort our baby and that I was a disgrace to them. My grandmother was no better, she told me to suck it up and pay for my crime. Her words to me were, you made your bed, now you have to lie in it, which looks like you already did. Calvin,

I was so broken, ashamed and alone. My parents told me that your trouble caught up with you and this is the life you would have tied me up in. They said, you got what you wanted, and you were done with me. Calvin said, "Now V, you know I asked you to marry me. I begged you to leave your family so we could start our own."

Victoria replied, "Calvin, after you were arrested, my parents constantly told me, I caused them even more embarrassment because I was involved with you. After they made me have the abortion, I went into a state of depression. All my parents ever did was live their lives as if I were not there, and when I was around, they treated me like I was such a bother. All I ever wanted was for them to accept me and love me. To this day, twelve years later, they still have not accepted me for the person I am. Well, except to brag to their rich friends."

Calvin said, "V, you never caused them any embarrassment, you were the most beautiful girl I had ever known, both inside and out. You were the best thing that ever happened to me. I have loved you since we were fourteen years old, the first day of middle school when I walked into that math class and saw you sitting in the front row, I fell in love instantly. Victoria said, "I fell in love with you at the same time as well Calvin, and I still love you." Calvin was silent, then he said in a stern voice, "It's getting late, I will call you at another time, I'm sure you need to get some rest since you are just getting back from vacation and all." Victoria

127

replied, "How did you know I was on vacation Calvin?" Calvin whispered softly, "Goodbye!" and hung up.

LYDIA

My New Reality

Although Lydia had the vacation of a lifetime, she is also excited to be back home. The island is exactly what she needed to relax and freely enjoy herself. She doesn't have to go back to work until Tuesday night, so she has some time to relax and get her thoughts together. She gets unpacked, does her laundry and just as she began to watch television, her cell phone rings, it's the hospital. She promised herself she would not answer but she decided to after all. It was the lead ER doctor, James Gulley. He was calling to see if she would come in. There had been a street fight and several victims had severe knife wounds, some were in critical condition.

They had a multi-car pileup earlier that evening, and they also had a couple of heart attack victims that arrived. He told her a couple doctors were out with the flu, so they were already short staffed. Lydia said, "Okay Jim, I will come right in."

Lydia gets dressed and heads into work. She drove her all white with tan interior 2019 Infinity QX50. After being on the island for a week, she wanted to get behind the wheel of her SUV and crank up the radio loud since she was going to be in chaos for the next ten to twelve hours. Upon arrival, there were two EMS pulling into ER. As soon as she parked, Dr. Jim called her again. She said, "I'm in the parking garage, I'm heading in." He replied, "Oh, Thank God because we just received two gunshot victims and they are both in critical condition." Lydia says, "I will be right there." Lydia is thinking to herself, *what in the world is going on in the city tonight? Oh, erase that thought, the city is always crazy.*

As soon as she arrives at the nurses' station, she takes charge of the chaotic emergency room. She assessed the patient's condition. She gave direction, where to send the most critical, and where to send the least critical. She asked one of the charge nurses to call and see who was on call for surgery and to get them in there. Lydia is examining a patient with several knife wounds to his lower abdomen. He is speaking in Spanish; Lydia can communicate with him. She asked him, if he could feel his legs and if he had pain, in any other area besides his stomach? The young man told her, yes, he also had severe pain in his lower back, and he has pain radiating down the back of his legs. She asked, if he had any alcohol or drugs in his system, he said, "I smoked a little pot today and I had a few beers." She thanked him for his honesty, as they were cleaning his wounds to check the severity of them. After getting him stabilized, he was sent to get an ultrasound and x-ray to determine if the knife damaged any of his internal organs.

She then went to the next room. It's a gunshot victim. He had a gunshot wound to his right shoulder; the bullet just missed his heart by a couple of inches. He had already been to x-ray, and they were preparing him for surgery to remove the bullet. After assessing and stabilizing several more critical patients, she enters another exam room, it's a lady in her late twenties, she is crying and complaining of head pain. Lydia looked at her chart and said, "Ms. Kingston," the lady replied, "You can call me Bridget." Bridget said she had a migraine headache that she had been dealing with since early morning. She explained to Lydia, she tried everything to get it to go away, but nothing was working. Upon examination, Lydia noticed the lady recently had stitches removed on the left side of her head. She asked, "How did you sustain that injury." Bridget replied, "I was getting out of the shower about a week ago, I lost my footing, I slipped and fell. I hit my head on the end of the bathroom vanity." Lydia asked, "Did you pass out?" Bridget replied, "Yes, my neighbor who lives below me said she heard a loud bang and when she came to my door and I did not answer, she knew something was terribly wrong and she called 911. The EMS brought me here."

Lydia asked, "Did they give you any medication for your headache?" She examines her eyes with the bright flashlight. Bridget replied, "Yes they did, I was doing great until I got dizzy and bumped my head on the door this morning." Lydia had concerns about Bridget's glossy eyes but as crazy as ER is right now, she just needed to get as many patients out of ER possible. Lydia said to Bridget, "I see here, you said your pain level on a scale of one to ten was an eight. Is that still correct?" Bridget replied, "The pain has gotten worse; especially, since you put that light in my eyes. So, it is now definitely a ten." Lydia goes ahead and prescribes her pain medicine, since her injury was valid. She is concerned, however, about the stoned look in Bridget's eyes. Lydia said, "Bridget, I'm going to prescribe you Vicodin and I want you to see your family doctor this week. I'm only going to…" Bridget cut her off in mid-sentence and said in an angry tone, "Vicodin sucks, it does nothing for me. Can't you give me something stronger?" Lydia exclaimed, "Well, for your injury, Vicodin should stop the pain. We can give you something in your IV, to get your pain under control. Do you have someone to drive you home?" Bridget said, "Yes, my sister will come to get me but I'm telling you Vicodin does not work for me, can you please give me something to stop my pain. I really need to go to work tomorrow. I would like to get a good night's sleep without this horrible headache keeping me up all night." Lydia agrees to prescribe her a stronger narcotic, but she told Bridget, she would not give her any medicine in her IV until someone arrived, to confirm taking her home. Bridget agreed.

Lydia was off to a few more critical patients. They rushed the young man with the knife wounds to his abdomen and lower back to surgery; his injuries were very severe. She finally gets a break as the ER was becoming more manageable. Lydia checks her messages on her cell, she notices a missed call from Sam. She smiles, as her thoughts go back to the great time they had at dinner and dancing last week. She promised, to call him when she returned but forgot when the hospital called and asked her to come in. She sneaks down a hallway and calls Sam back. He answers, "Hello beautiful!" He could feel her smile though the telephone. She said, "I'm sorry Sam, I meant to call you this evening, but the hospital called and asked me to come in because they were very short staffed." Sam replied, "I understand, they called me in tonight as well, I just finished up in surgery." She said, "Oh, now I feel much better knowing that you were not waiting on my call." Sam said, "I was anxiously waiting with my cell phone in my hand, staring at it saying, ring, ring." They laugh and talk about the great time they had and how much they enjoyed each other's company. Just as they were about to make plans to see each other, they paged Lydia on the intercom. Sam said, "Duty calls so I will call you in the morning. Maybe we can meet for breakfast after our shifts are over." Lydia smiles and says, "That would be awesome, I can't wait to see you." Sam replied, "Likewise, talk to you soon."

This was the shift from hell tonight. Lydia goes home and showers off the stench from tonight's shift. She wonders why she answered her phone, but deep down inside, she knows her commitment to the cause of being a doctor and she couldn't let her colleagues down or the patients. She is so looking forward to having breakfast with Mr. Handsome Sam, with the sexy voice. Lydia looks into her massive wall closet and her eyes settle on a black mid-thigh skirt; with black leggings, long black boots with a silver buckle by the ankles. A royal blue and black V-neck sweater with silver jewelry accessories, including a big bold silver bracelet. She must top off her outfit, with an all-black Kate Spade purse. She slipped on a lightweight wool cape and went to the parking garage to get her SUV.

When she entered the parking garage, she noticed a young lady that she had never seen before, parked adjacent from her parking spot. The lady was mid aged and professionally dressed. They made head gestures and said a polite hello to each other. Lydia noticed the lady was driving an Infinity SUV just as she, only the lady's truck was silver. "Humm," Lydia said as she entered her car. She was thinking, *she must have just moved while I was on vacation because I have never seen this car or that lady and I've been living here five years. Her outfit and accessories are designer. A label person, just like me!*

Lydia arrives at the cafe. As soon as she entered, Sam motioned her to his table. He pulled her chair out, took her cape, and placed it on the back of her chair. He gave her a polite peck on the cheek and said, as he was sitting back in his chair, "It is so nice to see your beautiful face again. It looks like the sunshine is still on your face from St. Lucia. You lit up the room as you entered." Lydia blushed. As beautiful as she is, she is still quite bashful. Lydia said, "Thank you and it is good to see you as well. How did your night turn out last night?"

Sam replied, "I spent three hours in surgery for one patient and two hours for another. The first patient had deep lacerations to his lower abdomen, it penetrated through his spleen and part of his kidney. The spleen was reparable, but I had to remove the kidney, we could not repair it. The second patient lost his pancreas. "

JAMISON

My New Reality

Jamison is getting dressed for the office this morning. He is excited about the new business he acquired with Lake Front Memorial. He must quickly start production to fill the open orders, thanks to Dr. Naomi's recommendation. He opens his oversized walk-in closet, pulls out a dark brown Italian suit and a dark brown shirt. He selects a brown poke-a-dot tie with tan and navy-blue speckles. His shoes are dark brown leather. He adds gold accessories to accompany the colors, grabs his leather strap brief case and heads out the door. He stops at the first floor to get a newspaper and coffee, from the coffee bar. Then heads down to the parking garage, to get his Pythonic Blue Metallic BMW X7 SUV.

Upon getting in the car, Jamison says, "Hello doll, I missed you!" He starts her up and heads to the office. As he is driving in the morning's thick traffic, he is thinking about his vacation and how exhausted he was from all the activities. Then he smiles, as he reminisces about the lady he connected with in St. Lucia. As much as he said he would not connect with her, he lost the battle within. They hooked up every night, from Tuesday through Friday. "Vanessa was her name; sweet, sweet Vanessa." The heavy traffic did not irritate Jamison this morning because all he could think about was the money he just made, with his newest invention. He calls Jade and leaves a voicemail message requesting to schedule an appointment with her to update his LLC, license his surgical instrument and to create a contract between his company and Lake Front Memorial regarding the purchase. Releasing him of all liability for any current or future operational errors. Something like errors and omissions coverage, to protect his company.

Jamison arrives at the office, and it's unusually quiet. The mornings he is not in surgery testing equipment, he is usually in the office quite early. This morning seems unusual, no one has arrived yet. He questions the day and says, "It is Monday, isn't it?" He checks the lab, and no one is in there. He proceeds to his office, he finds a note on his desk and on his white board, to come into the conference room at eight o'clock, for a meeting to recap the previous week. Since he had been on vacation last week, he thought nothing of it. He checks his emails and looked over his blueprints for a new design, he was working on. At seven fifty-five, Jamison arrives in the conference room, it was dark. *Strange,* he thought, and when he turned the lights on, everyone yelled SURPRISE!

They surprised Jamison, which is difficult to do. Nothing gets past this man, but this time, they surprised him. Jamison said, "What is this all about?" The owner of the company walked over to him and said, "Jamison, I am immensely proud of you. You have done an exceptional job and you always go above and beyond the scope of work. I wanted to give you a big celebratory welcome back when you returned from vacation. I just want you to know how much I appreciate you and all that you do for this firm." Jamison is overjoyed, as he flashes those perfect white teeth, this time his deep dimples show. He shakes his boss's hand, and his boss turns it into a hug. Everyone in the office comes around the large elaborate conference room and congratulate him on his success. They have a big breakfast catered in with lots of health food options to choose from. He had cards from his colleagues and one from his boss.

Jamison is somewhat a loner in the office. Therefore, it shocked him to see so many people come in early to congratulate him. He thought to himself, *what a way to return to the office from vacation.* After about an hour of commencing with his co-workers, Jamison goes to his office to catch up on his emails and phone messages. He opens the envelope from his boss; it's a bonus check for twenty-thousand dollars. He smiles and continues to work.

At noon, his cell phone rings, it's Jon, his name registered on the caller ID this time. Jon said, "Welcome back Jamison!" He replied, "Good afternoon Jon, and thank you." Jon exclaimed, "I hope you had a relaxing vacation because we have a lot to do this week. Are you ready to get started?" Jamison said, "I was born ready." Jon replied, "I'm glad to hear that, can we meet in Wicker Park this evening, around five thirty? " Jamison said, " Yes, I will be there." Jon said, "I will text you the address." Jamison, inhales a big deep breath and says to himself, *I can't' believe I'm doing this, but why not?*

Jamison was meeting Kendra, a lady friend for lunch at DOC B's on Grand Avenue. He met her one night at the BLVD. They have this relationship of no questions, no answers. They occasionally connect from time to time. They are both professionals and respect each other's privacy. She recently moved to the city while Jamison was on vacation. She is excited to tell him about her new place. Jamison really likes her, but he doesn't have time for a relationship; especially now that he has started a new life, he cannot share with anyone. He enters the restaurant and waits for her arrival. He made reservations so they wouldn't have to wait because of the busy lunch rush. Kendra drives a silver

Infinity SUV and parked right beside Jamison. She enters the restaurant, and it seems as if the entire place became still. She is tall, slender but curvy, full lips, bold eyes, her hair has a short sassy asymmetrical cut with tapered sides. She wears the top of her hair spiked. She looked like a model from the cover of Vogue magazine. She wore a silver ruffled blouse with off white slacks. A mother-of-pearl necklace, matching earrings and bracelet. Silver pumps and an oversized Michael Kors handbag. She was stunning! As their eyes connected, Jamison flashed his perfect white teeth so big, his dimples deeply sunk in.

They sat talking and catching up on each other's lives, as much as they are each willing to share. The most they knew about each other was their bedside manners and their careers. She knew that he was a successful robotic engineer, specializing in surgical tool designs, and he knew that she was a federal judge. They both agreed in the beginning of their connection, not to get personal or attached to each other. They laid down ground rules and for the past year; they have held up their end of the deal. Jamison is thinking about how Kendra's candy apple red lipstick is looking especially lovely this afternoon. He is having a hard time focusing on her words. Kendra asked Jamison, "So did you have a great vacation?" Jamison said, "It was magnificent." Kendra smiled and said how pleased she is to no longer have to drive an hour and a half into the city every day. Jamison said, "How was your move?" She told him how she had the movers pack, load, unload an unpack everything while she was in court. Jamison laughs and says, "It's like that?" She smiles and says, "Yes, it is, it's called the power of money."

The server comes over and takes their orders. They are both health conscious and each order the grilled chicken salads with corn, cilantro, tortilla strips with black bean drizzle, with spring water to drink. Jamison said, "How is work, is your caseload busy this week?" Kendra replied, "Not too bad, would you like to come over to see my new place sometime this week?" Jamison said, "I would love too." His deep dimples appear again. They enjoyed their lunch and each other's company, as they always did. They could spend weeks apart and come together as if it were yesterday. They had a deeper connection that neither one of them will embrace.

Jamison's phone vibrates in his pocket, it's the text message he was waiting for. He is the polite type of man and gave all his attention to Kendra. He did not look at his phone until they were in their separate vehicles and had pulled off the parking lot.

Jamison looks at this text message and it said Community Clinic of Wicker Park 46021 Division Street. Park in the back and text me when you arrive. Jamison replies got it. He is heading back to his office, and he receives a call from Dr. Naomi Lee, he answers, "Hello Doc." She tells him he will need to get a burner phone and to get it today before the meeting this evening. It cannot have GPS tracking and make sure it's from a service provider, he can reload using cash. No credit card transactions. She continues on to say, "Load a few hundred dollars on the phone and never use the same location twice. Once you have the new phone number, delete Jon's number and all text messages out of your personal phone. Every couple of months, you will destroy the phone and purchase another one, from a different location. Repeat the same process by loading it with cash only, of a few hundred dollars. Jon will fill you in with other details this evening." She hangs up.

Jamison arrives back at his office and works on his new design. Jade returns his call regarding the contract he needs prepared and the licensing of his new surgical tool. She asks if he could come by her office on Thursday of this week at ten a.m. Jamison checks his calendar and tells her that works for him. It is now three thirty, and he needs to go purchase the phone and do as Dr. Naomi said. He didn't want to purchase the phone near his work or his home, so he drove closer to Wicker Park and made the purchase. After getting the phone business squared away, he arrives at the clinic and parks in the back. He texts Jon *Here* from the new number. Then he deletes all of Jon's numbers and text messages from his personal phone. Jon opens the back door and Jamison enters the clinic. This clinic is exceptionally clean and has multiple exam rooms. It is fully staffed with nurses, office personnel and a receptionist. The lady nods her head at Jamison and smiles. Jamison nods his head and continues to walk with Jon down a long hallway, to a very large office. Dr. Naomi was sitting in the high back dark brown leather chair. She turned the chair around just as Jamison entered. She had a smile on her face, and this was the second time that Jamison had ever seen Dr. Naomi smile, in the five years of working with her. She says, "Welcome to the family Jamison. I presume you took care of the phone as instructed?" Jamison replied, "Of course." She smiled and said, "I knew you would. Now let's discuss business; especially the money."

Dr. Naomi tells Jamison he will need an alias name. She had chosen Jason for him. Jamison stated, "Jason it is." She gives him more details about the underground organ harvesting they run out of her clinic. Jon is her brother, who is the broker. He brings on clients with the big money that can afford to bypass the donor list. Jon is also a surgeon at Westgate Memorial hospital in Evanston. Dr. Naomi's husband is also a surgeon at Stonehedge Medical hospital, they all three perform the transplants there at the clinic. Dr. Naomi explains to him the supply and demand for organs, and how if you have money, you have power.

Jamison asked, "So where do these organs come from?" By this time, Dr. Naomi's husband enters her office, she introduces them. "Dr. Myung, this is Jamison." Dr. Myung nodded his head and shook Jamison's hand. Dr. Myung said, "Jamison, or should I say Jason, we finally meet. I see my wife is giving you the details." Jamison says, "Likewise and yes, she is somewhat filling me in." Dr. Naomi continues to explain to Jamison, how they misdiagnose some of their patients, by telling them, the organ is not functioning properly, or they have a tumor on the needed organ, after determining they are a match. My assistant, you saw her when you came in, at the front desk, is Dr. Myung's sister. She keeps detailed records of organs we need to find a match for. Because we are surgeons at three major hospitals, we do not have to keep our clients waiting very long. Jon just had a couple of patients with stab wounds last night, that were a match for a kidney and a pancreas, which are both high demand. The patient had a severed spleen from a knife fight and Jon told the patient that during surgery, they determined the kidney was beyond repair and they had to remove it to save his life.

Jon brought the organs here, and we successfully transplanted them to the new recipients last night." Jamison said nothing but nodded his head in deep thought. He finally asked, "So why do you need me, where do I come into this?" Dr. Naomi replied, "The supply and demand has increased, and we need someone to transport from Lake Front Memorial to the clinic. Since you and I are in surgeries together, and you are not on staff. It would not look suspicious for you to be in and out of the surgical area, as you have been the past five years. When you are not in surgery, we could say, you are collecting data for your new surgical instrument, which would give you a reason, to be at the hospital without question." Jamison says, "I see, and it looks like you have a well thought out plan." Dr. Naomi stated, "Since you have assisted me in surgery, or should I say observed me using your inventions, we could train you to assist in the transplants." Jamison asked, "How do you do a total organ transplant in a clinic?" Dr. Myung said, "Let's give you a tour of the operations." They get up and take Jamison on a tour. Afterwards, when they are back in Dr. Naomi's office, Jamison retorted, "You make enough money to fund this clinic, pay the staff, have enough left over to take care of expenses and divide the cut?" Dr. Naomi explained, the clinic is truly a clinic funded by government grants and municipal bonds. We also have several fundraisers each year, to help fund the clinic. Money is not a problem for the recipients because they are very wealthy, therefore, they can bypass the donor list. We will pay you four thousand dollars for every transport from Lake Front Memorial. We usually need three to four a week. We also have three to four organs per week from the other two hospitals.

They approach the operating room and Jamison is amazed at the state-of-the-art surgical equipment, just as the hospital has. Jamison asked, "What do you do about anesthesia?" Dr. Myung said, my cousin is an anesthesiologist and another anesthesiologist from Lake Front Memorial also comes to the clinic and assist in transplants. Jamison exclaimed, "Wow, you have a fantastic operation here. Where do I start?"

JADE

My New Reality

It's seven thirty in the morning, Jade is already at the law firm. She arrived early, to prepare for her meeting with Jamison, to amend his Limited Liability Company, and to license his new surgical tool. She has had a busy couple of days, working on depositions and discoveries for her new client. This new case load from Lake Front Memorial, is her number one client, so she did not have much time to work on Jamison's documents before their meeting this morning, at ten o'clock. She had one of the junior attorneys amended his LLC and prepare a contract between Jamison's company and Lake Front Memorial, so she only has to review it. As she was reading over the new contract, she notices the agreement was between Jamison's company and Lake Front Memorial as the buyer for his new surgical tool. "Humm", she says, "Looks like Jamison and I have a mutual client?" Her phone rings, it's her nephew Nicholas. She answers right away and says, "Hey, is everything okay" Nicholas says, "Auntie, it is not, papa is very ill and the doctors are not sure if he is going to make it through the week." He said to Jade, "Mom said she wrote you a letter to let you know he was sick, but he has gotten worse and you really need to come home to see him."

Jade was filled with rage, and said to Nicholas, "Sweetheart, I'm super busy with a big case right now and I cannot just drop everything and run back to Seattle like that." She was very gentle with him, especially now, that she knows, he is her little brother and not her nephew. Nicholas exclaimed, "I know you hate them, and you should, but he is very sick, and he has been asking for you." Jade replied, "Like I said dear, I cannot just leave right now. I have an important client I'm meeting with in about five minutes and I will call you later this evening." Nicholas asked, "Will you at least call papa or grandma to check on them? They would love to talk to you." Jade responded, "They have never liked me and I'm sure I'm the last person they want to hear from." She tells Nicholas she really must go now and will call him this evening. She tells him not to worry and to have a good day. She hangs up her cell phone and takes in a big deep breath. She tells herself to just keep breathing and get back to work.

Jamison arrives at nine fifty on the dot. He is waiting in the lobby, the receptionist calls Jade to see if she wanted to conduct the meeting in one of the conference rooms. Jade replies, "No, please send him in. Jamison enters, and says, "Ms. Alexander, what a pleasure to see you again." They always kept it professional, when they came to each other's office. This practice was a way to keep office chatter and rumors down. Jade tells her receptionist, "Thank you, that will be all." Once she leaves and closes the door. Jade laughs and says, "Ms. Alexander is my mother." Jamison laughs, and says, "I forgot how beautiful your office is," as he walks around the office and admires the views. Jade said, "Thank you, since I spend so much time here, I may as well make it welcoming and cozy. She says to Jamison, "I had one of our junior attorneys draft up your contract, I reviewed it this morning. Take a few minutes to look it over, to ensure it has all the details you wanted. We have listed the patent number for your instrument. I also had a no copyright clause added." Jamison is sitting at the small round conference table next to the window, he reads the contract a while, then his eyes stare out of the big window. He is in deep thought, then his eyes glare back at the contract.

Jade asks, "Is everything okay? Does it entail all the specifications you requested?" Jamison replies, "Yes, it looks great, and it covers everything." Jade said, "You looked like you were in deep thought. I just want to make sure; it is exactly what you want before you have Lake Front Memorial sign it. Look here at appendix C, I have specific wording listed that they are not to replicate, duplicate or sell the device to anyone or any institution." Jamison replied, "Yes, I see that here, thank you. That is the exact wording I needed." Jade asked, "What's wrong? You don't seem to be happy about the contract? You should be excited. This is what you were born to do, and that is to create instruments, that would change the way of the surgical world. You did it, Jamison! You did what you always dreamed you would do." Jade's excitement shows in her big smile. Jamison finally snaps out of his stench and says, "You are right, Jade. I'm just tired, it has been a long week, and it's only Wednesday."

Jade has a serious look on her face as she looks at Jamison and says, "Yes, it has been a long week, by the way, I have a question for you." Jamison looks up at her as they are sitting at the round conference table. Jade asked, "Do you know a Dr. Naomi Lee?" Jamison replied, "Well, I know that she is a surgeon at Lake Front Memorial, why do you ask?" Jade said, "No reason, I was simply curious because I had seen her name in the files as being the top transplant surgeon in the nation. I also remember reading; she was also an oncologist as well." Jamison replied, "Yes, she may be, I'm not sure? I just know, she is one of the surgeons who tested and approve my medical instrument. She was pleased with it and it was her evaluation that landed me the contract." Jade said, "Well that is wonderful; especially, since she is the top transplant surgeon and all. This could become big for you, Jamison. What if this is only the beginning and we are doing contracts for hospitals and clinics across the nation for your surgical tools? Jamison, this is Huge!" She stands up with excitement, and says again, "This is HUGE!" As she raises both hands up to her head and smiles at him. She then does a small spin and pulls him up out of the chair. She looks at him and exclaimed, "Do you realize how big this is?" Jamison smiled and nodded his head, but he had a look in his eyes, as if he was having an out-of-body experience. His mind was rethinking his decision to join Dr. Naomi and her team. He just realized he was on to something that would bring him in more, than a few thousand dollars for each delivery. Jade blurted, "Earth to Jamison." He smiles, looks at her and said, "We will celebrate big at the SPOT Friday night. I am excited Jade, I am tired, that's all. A lot has happened this week, and I have been a little restless. You are right Jade; this IS huge, and I need to be marketing this across the country."

Jade's receptionist buzzed, to let her know her eleven thirty appointment canceled. Jamison said, "Perfect, let me take you to lunch." Jade said, "I really should work through lunch today. This cancellation will help me catch up. "Jamison replied, "No, I'm taking you to lunch, so get your purse and let's go Ms. Alexander." She smiled and said, "Well since you put it that way, I guess I have no choice." They have a wonderful lunch at a cafe down the block from her law firm. Jamison thanks Jade for reminding him of how huge his invention is and how it will change the way surgical procedures are performed. Jade said, "I was starting to wonder, if you wanted the contract deal or not? I've never seen you look so puzzled. You are a man of certainty and you always know what you want." Jamison smiles and says, "You know me pretty well, don't you?" Jade says, "Yes, this little skinny scared girl knows you well." They laugh and enjoy their meal.

Jade is back at the firm, as she is riding the elevator to the twenty-sixth floor, she is thinking, she is so glad she took Jamison up on his offer for lunch. She always enjoys his company, and he seems to take a load off her mind when they are together. He is that big brother she never had that she could lean on. Jade went from a happy afternoon to a sad look in her eyes as she sat back down at her desk. She starts to think about Nicholas, and the phone call, the fact that he is her brother and doesn't even know it. She yells, "Dam them! Dam them, for all these years of deception."

Her computer beeped; it was her reminder for her three o'clock meeting. She switches her mood back to business mode, she fluffs her hair, check her makeup, grabs the files and heads to the conference room. This is their regular weekly, Wednesday staff meeting with all the attorneys and partners. Each associate goes over their cases files one at a time and the other associates discuss the case and make recommendations if needed. One of the junior associates has a case where the claimant is filing a case against Westgate Memorial hospital in Evanston, for the losing a kidney as a result from a car accident. This grabs Jade's attention!

CHAPTER SEVEN

Standing on the Mountain Top

VICTORIA

Standing on the Mountain Top

Victoria went to the casino after leaving the SPOT last night. She hit big, and I mean big. She won ten thousand dollars at one of the high rollers blackjack tables. Then she went to the slot machines and hit two jack pots. Five thousand dollars on one machine, and seven thousand on another machine. She was feeling like she was on top of the world right now; she was in a good place.

Since Victoria had consumed several martinis, she spent the night at the casino. She upgraded one of her free night stay to the presidential suite. She was escorted to her room by the hotel security because of the sizable sum of money she had just won. As they are getting off the elevator, Victoria has that uneasy feeling in her gut again. She looks around and doesn't see anyone on the floor. She was thinking, *maybe I have had too many drinks and I just need a good night's sleep.* She was now completely out of the hole and could put half of her winnings in savings and the other half back into her retirement account.

Once she was inside of her luxurious suite, the concierge made sure she was pleased with her room accommodations, which comprise of a wet bar, stocked pantry and ceiling to floor windows. The suite was fifteen stories, and she had a beautiful view of the city from the outskirts. Victoria is pleased with the accommodations. After the long roller coaster ride of her wins and losses, she ran herself a hot bath in the Jacuzzi tub. While the tub was filling up, she poured herself a glass of wine and stared out the window. She thought about Jamison and how his dream had now become a reality. She was so proud of him and his success. She was thinking to herself; *hard work brings success.* She was feeling proud of herself for being a successful female bank president, considering the path her life could have taken her because of her troubled childhood. She put her glass up to the window and made a toast to her reflection and says out loud, "Mom and dad, I made it. You couldn't break me!" A tear fell down one side of her cheek and then the other. She remembers the tub filling and hurried to check it. She catches it just in time. She turned on the radio to a nice jazz station and take a long hot bath with the jets on top speed.

This is the first time since St. Lucia, she is feeling relaxed. She can't get the conversation she had with Calvin last Sunday out of her head. She says with sadness, "He has not called this week." She cannot call him because his call was unknown, and he blocked his number. The things he said to her were heart breaking. All this time, she thought he had left her because he could not forgive her for having the abortion. She had no idea her parents, her father, had him falsely accused of dealing cocaine and had him arrested. She says out loud, "I wanted him to understand I had nothing to do with it, I did not even know this had happed to him!" As she cries and the tears are streaming down her face, and for the first time since the abortion, she has a big deep cry about losing her baby and Calvin. It has been twelve years, and she can't believe it feels like it just happened yesterday.

The next morning, Victoria wakes up to her cell phone ringing. It is Lydia, "Hey Victoria, are we still on for breakfast?" Victoria has a terrible headache and suddenly realizes she was not at her condo. She asked Lydia, "What time is it?" Lydia replied, "Eight thirty, are you still sleeping?" Victoria says, "Yes, but I didn't realize I had slept this late. Can we move it to lunch? "Lydia says, "Sure, I will go to the gym in the meantime, how about we meet at Jade's cafe around eleven thirty?" Victoria agrees. Victoria jumps up and realizes she only has the red after five dress from last night. She doesn't want to walk out of the hotel wearing it, and she certainly cannot wear it to meet Lydia for lunch. She doesn't have time to go home and change.

She quickly calls the concierge; she is thankful it is a female who answered. Victoria explains her situation and explains how she needs an outfit, a total wardrobe change, preferably a dress and a pair of shoes. She asked if there were any department stores nearby that would deliver to the hotel right away. The concierge said, "I will take care of it for you, Ms. Ellis. What would you like?" She gave her the size she needed and explained it needed to be something casual. She told her there would be a big tip for her, if she could make it happen within the hour. Victoria is in a panic because no one knows about her gambling obsession. She has kept this a secret for twelve years and plans to keep it that way. How would she explain a bank president with a gambling habit?

Fifty-five minute later, the concierge finally calls Victoria's room and says, "Ms. Ellis, I have your order, would you like me to bring it up now?" Victoria replies, "Yes, and thank you very much." Ten minutes later, the concierge knocks on the door with a few bags for Victoria to choose from. She explains how she will return whatever she does not like, to the store for her. Victoria is pleased with the entire selection and decides she will keep them all. She asked the concierge how much the total was. The concierge tells her, it's already paid in full. Victoria replied, "Oh! I forgot; my credit card is on file here at the casino." The concierge said, "No maim, we cannot use your card without prior authorization. They informed us upon delivery the bill was paid." Victoria asked, "How could that be? No one knows I'm here. You are the only person who knew I needed to purchase clothing?" The concierge stated, "Maim, I'm not sure, I was just instructed to bring these items to your room. Your bill has been paid in full." Victoria gives her a one-hundred-dollar tip and sends her on her way.

Victoria does not have time to fret over it right now because she has to get dressed quickly and get to the city to meet Lydia. Luckily, Victoria has beautiful skin and doesn't wear much makeup, so the lack of it today will not look suspicious. Victoria goes to the valet booth and has her vehicle brought around. She is still stirring over how her outfits were paid in full. It is now ten thirty, and she has exactly one hour to meet Lydia. Her SUV comes around and as she is getting in, she has that uneasy feeling again, as if someone is watching her. She brushes it off and drives off in a hurry.

"I love that dress" Lydia says to Victoria, Victoria smiles and says, "Thank you dear, have you been here long?" Lydia replied, "No, I actually just arrived about five minutes ago." Victoria said, "Oh good, I was worried about being late because of traffic." Victoria looks at Lydia and could see, she has that glow on her face again. Victoria says, "Lydia, did you meet a man?" Lydia smiled and said, "A man? No! I am too busy, and my work schedule is too complicated for a relationship." Victoria said, "I don't care how busy you are or how complicated your workload is, you have a man in your life somewhere. Is it one of those doctors at the hospital? Are you sneaking around in supply room closets or empty rooms, making out?" Lydia replied, "Victoria, you watch too much television. I never have time to even eat while on shift because third shift ER is so crazy." Victoria retorted, "I don't care what you say, you have a man somewhere!"

The server comes over to get their drink orders. They both order hot tea and look over the menu. They place their order and Lydia redirects the conversation to Bridget. She tells Victoria to tell her more about the changes she sees with Bridget. Victoria explained, "When Bridget first started working for me, a little over five years ago. She was bright, energetic and eager to learn everything she could about banking. She went from being a teller, to becoming my administrative assistant, in just a few short years. She has always done an excellent job for me and was very dependable until about six months ago." Lydia asked, "So what happened six months ago that caused the change in her behavior and work ethics?" The server brings their food to the table, and they stopped the conversation until the server left. Victoria continues and says, "She was in a terrible car accident. She had a broken hip, and a broken left arm. Her car was struck on the driver's side in the middle of an intersection. They airlifted Bridget to the hospital. Lydia says, "Wait, I believe they brought her to Lake Front Memorial." Victoria says," Yes, it is, and she was in pretty bad shape. It took months of rehabilitation before she could return to work." Lydia says, "Hum, I see! And how was her performance when she returned?" Victoria replied, "It was a very slow start, and she only returned three days a week, half days for the first two weeks, and then she started working half days five days a week. She did not return full time until about two months later." Lydia asked, "Did you notice a difference in her personality or attention span? Victoria said, "Well now that I think about it, some days she would nod off and or require lots of coffee but I contributed her tiredness to, returning to work full time and it was taking a lot out of her." Lydia asks, "Did her behavior change for the better or for the worst?" Victoria retorted slowly, "Well, now that I really think about it, her behavior has progressively changed for the worst." The server comes and removes their plates and asks if either of them would like any dessert. They are both so deep in conversation that they both reply, "No thank you," in unison."

Lydia says, "From what you are telling me, it sounds to me like Bridget has an addiction to her pain medication. Did she seek any kind of counseling when she had the accident?" Victoria said, "I really don't know, you know that kind of information is so confidential now days. I do know our Human Resources department offers it." Lydia said, "I will check her records at the hospital to see exactly what her injuries were and what course of treatment they gave her. Please do not tell anyone about our conversation as I am violating all the HIPPA laws by looking at her medial record." Victoria replies, "No worries, I am also violating HR Laws by discussing her with you. This will be our secret. We cannot even tell Jade and Jamison about this!" Lydia agrees.

LYDIA

Standing on the Mountain Top

As Lydia was preparing for tonight's shift, she started thinking about the wonderful evening she and Sam had yesterday. They visited a couple of museums, had a romantic candle-lite dinner, and then went to see a late movie. She hasn't been to a movie theater since college. She can't believe they ate so much candy and greasy buttered popcorn. She felt like a high school girl, going out on her first date. This man knows how to plan the perfect evening, and he is such a perfect gentleman. We have so much in common and it feels great. Just as Lydia is getting her keys to leave for work, her cell phone rings, it is Sam. He tells her to have a great night at work and that he would call her in the morning. Lydia smiles and heads out the door to the parking garage.

As she was walking toward her SUV. She runs into the mysterious new tenant who was parking adjacent to her parking spot. The lady exits her vehicle as Lydia was walking past, they speak, Lydia goes over to the lady and introduces herself. "Hello, I'm Lydia, are you new to the building?" The lady replied, "Yes, I moved in a couple of weeks ago, my name is Kendra." Lydia smiled and said, "Well welcome to our community; it's nice to meet you." Kendra replied, "My pleasure and thank you, have you lived here long?" Lydia said, "I've been here five years." Kendra said, "I hope to see you around sometime." Lydia replied, "Likewise, and it was very nice to meet you, Kendra."

Lydia heads to the hospital. She remembers she must investigate Bridget's medical file for Victoria and also check the files of Maria and her mother. Sam has totally taken her mind off that situation and she needs to find out if they are still in the hospital; but more importantly, where they live. She arrives at work and of course, the emergency room waiting room is full. Lydia heads to the locker room to change into her scrubs. She talks with the lead doctor to prioritize the patient's needs. They had everything from gunshot wounds, car accidents, stabbings, heart attacks, overdoses, falls, you name it. Lydia thought, *it is it a full moon tonight?*

After about four hours of non-stop madness, she has a few

minutes to look at the medical records. First, she pulls up Bridget's and confirms she did have a terrible car accident about six and a half months ago. It was bad! She had multiple surgeries to her left hip and thigh. She also suffered a broken color bone on the left side and incurred a head injury. Bridget spent three weeks in the hospital. They discharged her to a rehabilitation facility for intense physical therapy. Lydia could also see where Bridget has weekly visits to the emergency room for pain, especially in her back and neck. There are complaints listed that she refuses Vicodin and any pain medication that is not a high-power opioid. There are notes from several doctors stating her injuries are totally healed, and she should not need any high-power pain medications at this stage; especially five months after the injuries occurred. Just as Lydia suspected, it's documented by other doctors, who believe she has an opioid addiction, which can easily result from her injuries. Lydia is thinking, *Bridget needs help, but how do we get it for her? No one can find out I know her.*

Lydia hears her name over the intercom and has to closes Bridget's medical file. Before she enters exam room eight, she skimmed the nurse's report. The patient arrived with three nails in his forehead from a nail gun. Lydia walks into the examination room and sure enough, this man has three long nails above his eyebrows. The gentleman is calm but is in pain. Lydia said, "Mr. Miller, can you tell me how this happened?" The gentleman said his co-worker tried to kill him. His heart rate rose as he was telling the story about the argument they had. Lydia told him to take a deep, slow breath, and try to relax. She explained, they need to get x-rays to determine how deep the nails are. Mr. Miller repeatedly asked, "Can't you just pull them out?" Lydia replied, "I'm sorry sir, we cannot. We need to know how deep they are, first. Do you know how long the nails are?" Mr. Miller said, "We were using one and one-fourth inch nails while we were working on building a door frame in a new home construction." Billie and I had a disagreement about the process. We got into an argument and that son of a, I apologize for my language, Billie came at me, put the nail gun to my head and pulled the trigger three times. That son of, was trying to kill me. Lydia said, "The nurse will give you something for pain in your IV and we will also need to get lab work. I will be back after your x-rays.

Lydia walks out of the exam room and into the exam room next door. There is a petite woman, holding her stomach in severe abdominal pain. No one on staff tonight understands what she or her husband are saying. Lydia goes over to her exam room and speaks Korean, which settles the lady down. After conversing back and forth and a quick examination, Lydia determines this could be acute appendicitis, and she needs to go to radiology right away. She explains the process to the lady and her husband, they both agree to the testing. She orders lab work and tells them she will be back to check on them as soon as she has the test results.

Lydia goes to the nurses' station to check the files of the Ramirez family because she will be off duty in a couple of hours. She needed to check into this before the first shift personnel comes in. The file says Mrs. Ramirez is still in the hospital; she is no longer in a coma and will be discharge to a rehabilitation facility as soon as she is stable. Maria was discharged this week. The report says Mrs. Ramirez's husband has not left her side. Lydia finds out their address and discovers they live in Wicker Park. Lydia is thinking, *wow, you need a good income to live in that neighborhood. I wonder what Maria does for a living.* Lydia has anxiety all over again. She cannot figure out how they ended up in Chicago? She panics, her cell phone rings. She hears, "Hello beautiful, hope your night hasn't been too bad." Lydia smiles and says, "Hello Sam, you know just the right time to call, don't you." Sam replied, "I was just thinking about you and wanted to hear your voice before I head to work this morning." Lydia was being paged; Sam could hear her name over the intercom. He says, "Well, duty calls and I will talk with you later today." Lydia answers her page. It was for the Korean couple. She needed emergency surgery and they need her to explain the procedure so they could sign the consent forms. After they signed the consent forms and they sedated her. Day shift had come on and there were other doctors who spoke Korean to assist them after the surgery. Lydia is glad her shift was over and headed to the locker room to shower and change clothes. She doesn't like wearing scrubs in public.

She goes to the gym after leaving work, to burn off the candy and butter she put in her body Saturday night. She really enjoys hanging out with Sam, but he likes to stuff her with deserts and carbohydrates. She realizes she will have to step up her workout regimen if she continues to see him. Lydia is in the gym and notices Kendra running on the treadmill. Lydia is thinking, *out of all the high-end gyms in the neighborhood, how did they end up in the same one?* Lydia gets on the treadmill beside Kendra and said, "Good morning, I haven't seen you here before." Kendra replied, "I just joined a couple of weeks ago, when I moved to the city." Lydia said, "Oh! so where are you from?" Kendra replied, "I lived in Evanston for eight years. The hour and a half drive to the city for work every day, was becoming tiresome. Especially, when I worked long hours." Lydia asked, "What do you do for a living?" Kendra said, "I'm a federal judge." Lydia raises her eyebrows and said with excitement, "Wow, that's amazing! I'm overly impressed. I love meeting women in high-powered positions." Lydia has a puzzled look on her face and says, "You don't look like a judge." They laugh. Kendra asked, "What should a federal judge look like?" Lydia replied, "Oh, I didn't mean it, the way it sounded. It's just, when you hear the words federal judge, you think of an old white man, not a young, beautiful woman like yourself." Kendra smiled and said, "No offense taken, I get that reaction a lot, when I tell people that I am a federal judge." Lydia asked, "Don't you have to be old or in your late forties to become a federal judge? You just appear to be too young." Kendra replied, "Thank you! My father is a federal judge, in New York, so let's just say, I learned the ropes pretty early."

Kendra asked Lydia, what does she do for a living? Lydia tells her she is a surgeon at Lake Front Memorial and works in the emergency room, third shift. Kendra smiles and says, "Wow, I never pictured you as a surgeon." Lydia says, "Why do you say that?" Kendra answered, "Because you look like a runway model; every time I see you in the parking garage, you look like you are heading to do a photo shoot." They both laugh and agree to connect soon.

JAMISON

Standing on the Mountain Top

Jamison is heading home from Wicker Park; he has been there every day since last week. The underground business is booming. Jamison is in deep thought as he is driving. *Wow, I never thought the underground business was like this? I knew there was a black market for organ transplants, but I never knew this is how it went down. I mean, people are paying tens of thousand dollars for a kidney. Heck, I've transported eight kidneys this week. I must admit, Dr. Naomi is a very smart lady. She had me purchase a small sprinter van and have a logo put on it that says, JH medical supply company. This way, it looks like I am delivering or picking up medical supplies for the clinic. We filled the back of the van with medical equipment such as ultrasound machines, gurneys, lab tables, exam tables, surgical instruments. Myung incorporated the name of the company, so it has a legal record of its existence and I'm being trained to assist in surgeries. Wow! I would have never seen myself as a surgeon.*

From the time Jamison was a little boy, he wanted to be an engineer like his father. His father taught him so much as a young child, so college courses were a breeze for him. He studied anatomy and physiology so he could specialize his robotics degree to design surgically assisted instruments. Jamison chose this career path because as a young child, he had to watch his mother's health decline because of kidney failure. They were constantly in and out of hospitals because she also had congestive heart failure. She had to frequentlhy have fluid removed off her lungs so she could breathe. She also went periodically because the port in her arm would get clogged often from dialysis treatment. Jamison thought, *I miss my mama so much. I so regret not being there when she passed away. I never got to tell her goodbye. My mistake cost me to lose a year and a half with my mama. I have so many regrets, but mama, I'm doing this for you. I will make sure that anyone who can afford it will not have to be on that extensive waiting list. Jamison sorrowfully says,* "I'm so sorry mama, I'm so sorry I let my temper get the best of me and I couldn't be with you, when you took your last breath."

He arrives at the gym to burn off his frustration and guilt. He switches his thoughts to the past week and all the money he has made. His firm thinks he is out doing demos for new potential surgeons at nearby surrounding hospital. When he is actually transporting organs from two, sometimes three, different hospitals to the clinic in Wicker Park. Jamison is hitting the weights extremely hard, and he is sweating profusely, when the annoying young man comes over and says, "Hey man, I've been looking for you?" Jamison rises with a wet face which hid the wrinkles in his forehead, and he retorted, "Why are you looking for me, young blood?" The anxious young man said, "I want to show you how much I can bench press now. I have been working very hard on it, and I can bench press as much as you now." Jamison is now even more annoyed. He wipes his face with a towel and says to the young man. "Is that right!" Jamison entertains the young man and watched him do fifteen repetitions. He then, gave the young man a few pointers on his stance and positioning. The young man smiles with excitement, Jamison says to him, "Keep your eyes peeled, young blood." Jamison walked over to the treadmill. He puts on his headphones, turned the volume on high and started a slow jog to warm up. Since Fall is ending and Winter is kicking in, he has to do his running on the treadmill now.

He is thinking about Kendra and the experience they had the other night. He is toying with the thought of calling her to meet him for lunch today. He realizes he is breaking his own rule, and he is developing feelings for her. Life is good, he tells himself. His career is more successful than he imagined it would be, at age thirty. He has patents and licensing for his surgical instruments. His firm is happy with the revenue and new clients he has acquired. Jamison smiles, and says, "Life is good!" He completes a ten-mile run and heads to the gentleman's room to shower and get dressed.

He checked the burner phone for messages, and sure enough, there is a message from Dr. Naomi which said, *"Jason, it is time to make the change today, try to do it this morning and let me know when it's completed."* Jamison knows this means it is time to change the burner phone out for a new one. Since business is heavier than expected, Dr. Naomi requested him to destroy the phone and to purchase a new phone every week. Jamison destroys the phone by removing the chip, smash it into tiny pieces, and dump the particles all over the city. He has a friend in the cremation business, so he runs the rest through the crematory. Dr. Naomi was extremely specific in the beginning, to make sure his fingerprints are not traceable to any parts of the phone. When he gets the new phone, he is to text the words, *thank you,* and they would all know to lock in the new number.

He heads home to get some rest. He needs to arrive to the firm early tomorrow. He has to prepare for the weekly staff meeting, go over some notes, check his emails and messages. The weekly staff meeting consists of the normal project jargon and who is working on what, with whom? What new client has come on board and or how can we increase business with our existing clients. The sales team is also usually present, which makes it last longer than it should.

Jamison arrives to the conference room, five minutes early as usual and a few of his colleagues right behind him. After everyone goes over their project needs and assignments, the meeting usually ends. This time, the president and CFO are present. The president looks over at Jamison and asks him to remain in the conference room for a quick meeting. He tells Jamison how much they value him and how grateful he is to have a senior engineer such as himself with so much talent at his firm. They offered him a position on the executive management team. He would oversee the design and production team and would report directly to him. Jamison is surprised, this is the position he has worked so hard for. He can't believe this is happening. He exclaimed, "Thank you sir, I won't let you down." Jamison's says, "We will move your office to the executive wing, you will have the same perks and advantages as the executives. We are having lunch today in the executive conference room, to fill you in on some of your new roles, responsibilities and new salary." Jamison smiles and says, "Thank you sir I will clear my schedule this afternoon." He heads to his office to prepare for the lunch meeting. He is so excited he is about to jump out of his skin. He can't believe what just happened. He never saw it coming, which is surprising because Jamison doesn't miss a beat.

He is thinking, how glad he is, he didn't call Kendra for lunch.

He is also thinking about how his extra responsibilities will require more of his time. How he can barely keep up now, with the underground business being so demanding. How will he manage his new role? He shakes it off and gets in celebration mode. He is thinking, *life is good!*

Jamison heads home after an exhausting workday. He enters his condo and says, "Home sweet home!" He sorts through his mail, while making a whiskey neat. He turns on the radio, to an upbeat hip hop station. Jamison is thinking about how happy he is with his life right now. His cell phone rings. It is his father. "Hello son." Jamison replies, "Hello dad, how are you and mom?" His dad answers, "We are doing well, son. I was just checking on you since you don't call your old man these days." Jamison said, "Sorry dad, I have been so busy with work. I just received a promotion today to join the executive management staff." His dad says, "Whaatt Boy! I knew you would do great things with your career. I'm so proud of you, son. I wished your brother would get his life together." Jamison went from being happy and excited, to that dark place deep in his soul, the place he doesn't like to think about. Jamison says, "Dad, do we really have to talk about him now? I have had an outstanding day, and I wanted to celebrate my promotion, with positive energy." Jamison's dad replies, "I can respect that son, we will save that conversation for another day. Did you find a good woman to settle down with yet?" Jamison laughs and says, "There you go again." They both laugh. His dad says, "I am so proud of the man you have become, son. Your mother was already proud of you, and I know she is smiling in heaven right now." Jamison said, in a slow tone, "Yes she is dad. I was thinking about her this morning and how I should have been by her side." His father said, "You have to stop beating yourself up over your past son, it was an accident and you have to forgive yourself." Jamison replies, 'I know, but it's hard." Jamison's dad says, "Son, enjoy the rest of your evening and be happy. You are in a good place in your life right now. I just want you to be happy and find that woman who is going to give me some grand babies." They laugh, Jamison's dad ends the call with, "Keep your eyes peeled son!"

JADE

Standing on the Mountain Top

Jade has a big court case for Lake Front Memorial today. The plaintive filed a complaint, alleging negligent medical care. She did not want to settle out of court and wanted to take it to trial. The prosecuting attorney's argument is; six months ago, they removed the claimant's left kidney because of a cancerous tumor. She then went through several months of chemotherapy and radiation treatments. After the treatments ended, she was told that she was cancer free. The claimant is twenty-two years old, and she does not have a family history of cancer. Because of the kidney being removed and the chemotherapy treatments, the plaintive stated, she now has to take several medications every day, lost time off work, lost wages, loss of hair and also the inability to have a baby. The prosecutor was requesting Dr. Naomi Lee to lose her license to practice medicine because of negligence and medical malpractice. They were suing Lake Front Memorial Hospital for four point eight million dollars.

The attorneys argued back and forth in the courtroom. They each had expert medical witnesses for their respective sides. Lake Front Memorial could produce radiology reports and x-rays showing the said tumor on the left kidney. They had laboratory results that showed cancerous cells. The prosecutor was first to state his closing argument on behalf of the plaintiff. Jade, as the defense attorney for Lake Front Memorial, said to the jury in her closing argument, "The plaintive had an undesirable outcome from a life saving procedure. Dr. Naomi Lee is the top transplant and oncology doctor in the United States. Lake Front Memorial Hospital, and Dr. Naomi Lee are not liable for any negligence or malpractice. The plaintive was fully informed and made aware of the risk, possible complication of the surgery and treatment. There was no deviation of the standard of care that caused harm to the patient. We have signed consent forms by the plaintiff, authorizing the surgical removal of the kidney because of a large cancerous mass. Due to the lack of expert testimony, showing any action or inactions by the defendants caused the plaintiff harm, I ask the court to dismiss the plaintiff's claim. The physician, Dr. Naomi

Lee, and Lake Front Memorial Hospital should not face any liability because the plaintiff experienced an unfortunate outcome." She walked back to her seat, next to Dr. Naomi Lee and the hospital administrator. They waited for the Judge to announce the time to return for the verdict.

Dr. Naomi Lee looked at Jade and said, "You are good! You are exceptionally good." Jade looked at her and smiled, with no response. Finally, the judge said, "We will return at two thirty for the verdict, the court is adjourned." Dr. Naomi and the hospital administrator dashed out of the courtroom and disappeared down the hallway. Jade was feeling particularly good about her closing argument and a little uneasy about being on the same side as Dr. Naomi Lee. It was something about her, she just didn't like; especially after meeting with her several times, to take depositions for the trial. Jade thought it was Dr. Naomi Lee's snooty presence, the way she appears to look down on others, that gave her the uneasiness, but now she believes that isn't it. Jade went back to her office until it was time to return at two thirty.

During her drive back to her firm, her cell phone rings. It is her boss, Mr. Stern, he says, "Jade!" She answers, "Yes!" He says, "I was told you did an outstanding closing argument in court this morning. That I should be very pleased with your representation of the firm." Jade sits up straight in her seat, as if she were looking over the hood of her SUV. She replies, "Sir, we just walked out of court. How do you know about my closing argument already?"

Mr. Stern said, "I would not be a senior partner if I didn't know these things. Keep up the great work, you are doing a magnificent job." He hangs up and Jade is smiling from ear to ear. This is a joyful moment for her. She shakes off the ill feelings from Dr. Naomi Lee and says to herself, "I may not like her, but it is she who will make me partner at the firm."

It's two thirty and all are present in the courtroom. Jade looks around the courtroom to see if she recognizes anyone from her firm. She does not see anyone; and she's still wondering how Mr. Stern found out so quickly about her closing argument this morning. The judge hits the mallet three times. He says to the jurors, "Do we have a verdict yet?" The lead juror stands up and says, "Yes, your honor, we do." The Judge said, "Read the verdict, please." The juror says, "Your honor, we find the defendants Lake Front Memorial Hospital and Dr. Naomi Lee not guilty of any negligence or malpractice in the case against the plaintiff." Jade smiles with excitement and attempts to hug Dr. Naomi Lee, but she saw the look in her eyes that read don't touch me. Although Dr. Naomi did not say a word, nor did she have a concerned look during the entire trial, Jade could read her body language, and simply said, "Congratulations Dr. Lee." Jade picked up her files and briefcase and walked out of the courtroom.

Jade returns to the law firm, excited about her big win. She is sitting at her desk and there's a knock on her door. It's four thirty and most of the staff usually starts leaving the office for the day.

She says, "Come in!" It's Mr. Stern, he has a big smile on his face and said congratulations. He has a bottle of bourbon and two glasses in his hand. He goes over to the round conference table by the window, opens the bottle and pours both glasses half full. He says, "Jade, I have watched you work extremely hard for this firm over the past four years and you have done an exceptional job. This toast is to you and your future here. Job well done today!" They toast, he downs his glass of bourbon, leaves the bottle with Jade and exits building.

Jade is sitting there with the bottle of bourbon, thinking about the great place she is in right now. She is finally relaxing and enjoying the moment. She takes her glass and walks around her office in admiration. She says to herself, "Not bad for a little shy girl, from a broken home and years of abuse. I made something of myself, even though the odds were against me." She runs her hands down the bookshelves, then across her elaborate desk that she special ordered. She stares out of the window that overlooks the city's skyline, takes in a deep breath, exhales slowly, releasing the negative energy and says out loud, "Mom, dad, I made it, despite your help or encouragement. Despite all the times you told me I would never amount to anything, I made it!" She fills her glass again half full, sits at her desk and calls Victoria to hook up Lydia who connected Jamison. She tells them about winning the big court case today. They squealed with excitement. Jade told them we will celebrate at the SPOT Friday night. Jamison acted just as surprised as the others. He congratulated her, as if he didn't already know. Dr. Naomi had mentioned to him and Jon that she had to go to court, and she didn't have a doubt in her mind, she would not win the case. She bragged about being that good at covering her tracks. Jade hung up, laid her head back in her big leather extra wide chair and took another deep breath. She held her glass up and made a toast to herself, and says, "I made it."

She gathers her purse, and for the first time in months, she leaves all the case files at her office and walks out. Jade stops by a cafe close to her office to order dinner. She is seated at a table in the back of the restaurant. While she is looking over the menu, the server comes over to take her drink order. She orders a decaf coffee and continues to look at the menu. Moments later, the server comes back to the table with her coffee and takes her food order. Jade is hungry, she does not remember having lunch today, and she only had a muffin at breakfast. She was so busy with the trial that she totally forgot to eat.

Just as the server leaves to put in her order, a beautiful lady comes over to Jade's table. Jade noticed her sitting in the restaurant when she entered but didn't give it any thought. The lady approach Jade and says, "You are Jace Alexander." Jade looks up and says, "Yes!" With a puzzled look on her face. Jade asked, "Have we met before?" The lady extends her hand to Jade and says, "No, we have not officially met, but I saw you in action this morning in court. My name is Kendra Mason." Jade shakes her hand and says, "It's nice to meet you Kendra." Kendra retorted, "You are very good you know!" Jade replies, "Thank you very much, I was nervous because of the large compensatory damage." Kendra said," It didn't look that way at all. You looked confident, and you controlled the courtroom." Jade said, "Thank you again." The server came back to the table with her food order. Kendra said, "I didn't mean to interrupt your dinner. I just wanted to stop and tell you how great you were this morning." Kendra walks away, Jade is feeling like she just won the lottery.

CHAPTER EIGHT

The SPOT

FRIDAY NIGHT

Victoria is home getting dressed to go to the SPOT tonight. She just finished her shower and goes to her oversized walk-in closet and retrieves a winter white dress. She is feeling good tonight, since the audit went well, and Bridget has come to work every day this week. She is very happy to see Bridget is making an improvement in her attendance and in her work performance. She really likes Bridget and does not want to let her go. She feels a connection with her, but doesn't understand why? Victoria's cell phone rings, it is an unknown caller. She is not sure if she should answer it or not; she has a feeling it is Calvin. No one else calls her unknown. She answers hesitantly, "Hello!" With excitement. The voice replied, "Hello Victoria, it's Calvin." Victoria says, "Calvin, how are you doing? I was hoping you would call again." Calvin replied, "I have been thinking about our conversation and I apologize for not allowing you to respond entirely. I apologize for cutting you off. I'm still very bitter about the whole situation, it still seems surreal to me. I lost years of my youth that I should not have lost." Victoria says, "I'm so sorry Calvin, I had no idea, I thought you left me because I had the abortion, I have always loved you and always will." Calvin says, "I believe you, V, I have had some time to think about our conversation and I believe you had no idea." Victoria asked, "Are you still in California? I didn't have a chance to ask you the last time we spoke." He said, "No, after my release from prison, I never returned; just as you." Victoria asked, "Can we meet up sometime? I'm not sure where you are but I live in Chicago now." Calvin was silent and then said, "In time, we will connect. I don't want to keep you on the phone, I know you are a busy lady, being a bank president and all." That kind of slipped out of his mouth. Victoria said, "I'm never too busy to talk to you Calvin, we have so much to catch up on." Calvin said, "Goodbye Victoria." and hung up.

Victoria sheds a small tear. She is sad for a short while, but then she quickly snapped out of it. Something she had learned to do since childhood. Her parents were never attentive to her and they would often disappoint her, so she learned how to shake it off and carry on. She pulls out her winter white pumps and adds silver accessories. Instead of driving, she calls an Uber, so she doesn't end up at the casino tonight.

She arrives at the SPOT about ten minutes early and Jade is already there. Victoria heads over to the table with a huge smile on her face to greet Jade and squeals, "Congratulations on your big win this week." Jade is wearing all black and her hair is hanging on her shoulders and straightened for once. Victoria says to Jade, "I love your hair like that. You look stunning." Jade smiles and says, "Thank you! You are killing that dress tonight." Victoria takes a seat; the server comes over right away with her apple martini. Victoria says to the server, "Thank you very much and keep them coming." Jade looks at her and asked, "Rough week?" Victoria replies, "Not really."

Lydia walks in wearing a navy-blue jump suite. Tonight, she looks like a runway model for sure. Jade looks up and exclaims, "Dam Lydia!" Victoria said, "You are right Jade, she looks amazing, doesn't she!" Lydia greets them both and says, "This may be a whiskey neat night tonight?" Jade looks at her with wide eyes and says, "Did you just say whiskey neat?" as they burst out in laughter. She orders a cosmopolitan instead. They ask Lydia about her week. She exclaims, "It was great, I find myself in a good place right now and it feels a little weird." Victoria and Jade both agree, they feel the same way. They ask, where is Jamison? It's past eight o'clock, and it is not like him to be late. Neither of them had heard from him and were starting to get concerned. Victoria calls his cell; he does not answer. She has a worried look on her face, Jade says, "Hey, I'm sure he is fine. He may have gotten tied up in traffic, but he will be here. You know Jamison has never let us down." Victoria relaxes and says, "You are right! You know me being the mother hen and always worrying." Lydia said, "That is why we need to have a toast to us!" They each hold their glasses up and say in unison, "To us!" Jamison comes over to the table with his drink in his hand and says, "Yes to us!" Victoria retorts, "We were getting worried about you." Jade said, "No, Victoria, you were getting worried, Lydia, and I knew that you would be here."

As Jamison took his seat, Victoria had that uneasy feeling again, but this time it was like a frigid wind blew past her and gave her a chill. This time was quite different. She now realizes she has this feeling at the casino and at the SPOT. Lydia says, "Victoria, are you okay?" Jade said, "You looked like you seen a ghost." Victoria said, "No, I just remembered something I have to do at work, that's all." She smiled and said, "Since Jamison has his drink, let's celebrate Jade with a toast to her big win in the courtroom." They each put their drinks in the air and exclaimed, "To Jade!" The server was already there with the second round, and places them on the table. Jade then says, "No, let's toast to us and our friendship, I don't know where I would be without you all. You have made such a positive impact on my life." She has a kind of sad look in her eyes. Jamison retorts, "Hey! To good times! We are not going to that dark place tonight." Lydia said, "You are right, let's celebrate to being in a good place in our lives tonight." Victoria looks over her shoulder. She sees a gentleman that resembles the one she had seen at the casino the other night. The one who reminded her of Calvin. Her head almost spins around trying to get a good look at him. The other three are so busy celebrating each other, they did not notice the concerned look on her face. She suddenly starts to think, *Calvin did not say where he lived? Just that he never went back to San Mateo. I wonder if he is here in Chicago.*

Jamison tells the ladies about his promotion to the executive staff and now will oversee the junior engineers in his firm. He tells them he may not be as available, because of his new workload. He uses all kinds of excuses of mentoring the new hires and keeping up with his current responsibilities. This is just to throw them off because the underground work has increased. Plus, he is spending more time with Kendra than he had ever planned. The ladies tell Jamison how proud they are of him and to do what he has to do. Just try to keep the SPOT open for their usual Friday night gatherings. Victoria tells Jamison, "We promised to never get so busy, that we can't meet up, once a week. For twelve years, we have made good on that promise to each other." Jamison says, "I will let nothing impede our Friday nights." They all toast and talk about how great their week was and celebrate where they are in their careers.

Jamison is feeling guilty for lying to his best friends about being so busy at the firm, when actually, he is super busy at the clinic. Jamison hands Jade an envelope after they have eaten their dinner. It is a card and a five-thousand-dollar gift card to Neiman Marcus. Jade's eyes light up and she says, "Jamison, I can't accept this!" Lydia said, "Yes you can, it's from all of us. We wanted to do something nice for you for your big win. We are so proud of you, Jade. The little shy girl has come out of her shell." Jade sheds a tiny tear and says, "I love you guys."

The band is playing one of their favorite songs. It's as if the music was from their personal play list tonight. They each got up to dance, just as they often did on Friday nights. Life is good!

CHAPTER NINE

Things Aren't As They Seem

VICTORIA

Things Aren't as They Seem

Victoria has had a heck of a week at the bank. They have been busy engaging in community events to gain new customer accounts before the year end. They have set up booths in the mall, grocery stores, health fairs, the Bears football stadium and colleges. Bridget has, surprisingly, been to work every day this week. She has attended every community event and has been a stellar employee. For the first time in the past six months, Bridget is doing a magnificent job and is back to her old self. As they were taking down the booth and packing up, Bridget and Victoria talked about life outside of work. This is the first time they have ever asked personal questions of each other. Victoria's rule is, there is a fine line between professional and personal conduct. Personal was not permitted at the bank during business hours. This time was an exception, since she initiated the conversation with Bridget. Victoria asked, "So, Bridget, are you originally from Chicago?" Bridget replies, "No, my parents moved here from California when I was a child." Victoria exclaimed, "What part of California, that is where I am from?" Bridget answered and said, "I'm from Santa Monica." Victoria replied, "I'm originally from San Mateo." Bridget sounded surprised and said, "Wow! You are from the Bay area? All this time, I never knew that. What a small world." Victoria says, "Yes, it is a small world!" She then asks Bridget, "Do you still have relatives there?" Bridget says, "Yes, we have relatives all over California, both of my parents come from large families, but we are the only ones here in Chicago." Victoria said, "It must have been hard to leave everyone behind and come to a strange city." Bridget replies, "It may have been for my parents, but I was a child, so this is all I know. I mean, we go back home a couple times a year to visit and I love the warm climate, but Chicago is home for me." Victoria said, "Yes, Chicago is home for me as well." Bridget said, "May I ask what brought you to the Windy City?" Victoria replied, "I needed a change of scenery and North Western University was the first college to offer me an academic scholarship and an acceptance letter." They laughed as they load Victoria's SUV with the event displays, brochures and banners.

Victoria asks Bridget if she wanted to grab dinner since it was so late, it would be her treat. Bridget replied, "Yes, that would be nice." They went to a small family-owned restaurant hidden in the neighborhood. The food was amazing, and they had great conversations. Victoria said to Bridget, "I am so glad you are making a full recovery from your car accident. I was genuinely concerned about you. You have come such a long way." Bridget says, "God is good and I'm so grateful to be alive." Bridget changes the conversation back to Victoria and says, "May I ask, do you go back to San Mateo to visit?" Victoria replied, "Rarely, my life is here now." Bridget asked, "So do you have relatives back home?" Victoria felt a little uneasy with this question and said, "Yes, I have lots of family back home, but because of my work schedule, it is difficult to find time to visit." Bridget then asks Victoria, "So, what does a bank president do for fun?" Victoria tells her, she enjoys shopping and spending time with her best friends from college. Bridge says, "Oh yeah, Jamison, Lydia and Jade." I've heard you speak of them over the years and they come to the annual Christmas party, I mean year end party, every year. Suddenly, Bridget remembers Lydia from the emergency room and panics. Lydia just treated her last week and prescribed her pain meds, and she thinks Victoria knows. She tells Victoria she does not feel very well and thinks maybe she should go home and lie down. Victoria offers to take her home, but Bridget says, she will call an Uber and besides, her car is at the bank. Victoria understands and tells her she hopes she feels better and to get some rest.

After Bridget leaves, Victoria is thinking, hum, *that was kind of strange. We were having an enjoyable conversation and out of nowhere; she is suddenly ill. I wonder what that was all about?* The server brings the bill, after she gives the server her credit card, Victoria's cell phone ring. It's that unknown caller again. Victoria answers, "Hello Calvin!" He says, "Hello gorgeous!" For the first time, his voice is soft, relaxed and not the usual hostile tone. Victoria says, "How are you?" He replies, "I'm good, I have finally come to terms with my life as it is. I have accepted the hand I was dealt." Then he blurts, "And before you say you are sorry, let's move on. No more apologizing. If you hate your parents as much as you say you do, you can join me in getting revenge on them." Victoria was silent for about thirty seconds, Calvin said, "Are you still there?" Victoria replied, "Yes, I am and yes, I would love to get revenge on them. I can't say they ruined my life, because the way they treated me prepared me for life as it is now. It just made me stronger." Calvin replied, "Stay tuned, I will fill you in on the details later this week." Victoria said softly, "Calvin, where are you? Are you still in California?" He replied, "Like I said, I have never gone back there. My mom passed away while was serving time for a crime I didn't commit. I really don't have a reason to go back, except to make your parents pay for all the years I lost." Victoria asked, "But where are you? I would like to see you." He answers, "Just know that I am closer than you think!" And he hangs up.

Victoria gathers her things and leaves the restaurant. As she is driving, she is heavy in thought about Calvin's conversation. She had every intention of going home but ends up at the casino. It is like her car is on autopilot and drove itself there. She is sitting in valet parking, fighting with herself on if she should go in or not. She had promised herself, after her big win, that she would not go back. She is at a good place in her life and she promised herself she would stop gambling.

She enters the casino and goes straight to the blackjack table. She was drawn to it by an inner force that was too deep to fight off. She loses one hand after another, then another. Suddenly, she is down by fifteen thousand dollars. She goes to the credit counter and writes a check for five thousand dollars to continue playing. It's like she can't stop, she must feel the velvet on the tables and feel the cards slipping through her fingers. It is a fix for her craving, and she can't resist. She loses again and is devastated. She goes back to the credit counter. This time, she gets a cash advance on her credit card for five thousand dollars. She goes over to the high roller table, which cost a hundred dollars a hand. While sitting there, she feels a presence around her, that uneasy feeling again. Her mind is racing about her conversation with Calvin about her parents. She loses the entire five thousand dollars.

She gets up to go to the bathroom to pull herself together and she notices a man that resembles Calvin. This time she follows him by playing different slot machines, so she doesn't look too obvious. She moves as the man moves, to kind of spy on him. He heads towards the back of the casino. She was hiding behind one of the slot machines. She was bobbing and weaving through the aisles, to prevent him from seeing her. As he turns around to greet a young woman, she could finally get a good look at him. Her eyes were about to fall out of her head, as she watched Calvin and Bridget talking to each other. They had a serious look on their faces. Victoria was thinking, *Oh my God! That explains all the questions about my hometown this evening and the sudden need for her to leave because she wasn't feeling well. Oh, they have played me! I wonder how they know each other.* She exclaimed, "They set me up!"

Victoria is so upset; she could barely contain herself. She rushed to the valet parking booth to have her SUV pulled up. While waiting, she is trying hard to keep from crying. Between losing twenty thousand dollars, seeing Calvin, her first love with that sneaky lying Bridget. Victoria is about to explode. Her SUV arrives, and she speeds off in a hurry. She is driving so fast; she ran right through a red light. Out of nowhere, a semi-truck with a trailer slammed into her SUV, on the passenger side. All the airbags deployed; Victoria is pinned in the vehicle.

LYDIA

Things Aren't as They Seem

Her mind is racing with thoughts of how the emergency room has been crazy tonight. It must be a full moon because this entire day has been crazy. Sam is being so secretive. We promised to be open and honest with each other, and for the past few months, things have been great. Lately, he has been very distant and secretive. He only wants to come to my place. He has been bringing dinner or breakfast to keep from going out in public. When I mention it to him, his excuses are being tired from back-to-back surgeries and being on his feet all day. At first, I was okay with that excuse, but I have this gut feeling, it is more to it than that.

A nurse says, "Dr. Sanchez, we need you in exam room three please." Lydia walks swiftly with the nurse, to get filled in on the patient in room three. The nurse says, "The patient is a thirty-year-old female, with what appears to be an infection, from a recent surgery of her left hip. The area is very red and swollen. It needs more attention than a topical ointment. We have started an IV but need you to examine the infected area." As Lydia puts on gloves and enters the room, her heart stops. She and the patient lock eye, and it stops Lydia in her tracks. The nurse says, "Dr. Sanchez, this is Maria Ramirez. She was in a car accident a few months ago that resulted in a broken left hip." Lydia says, "Hello Ms. Ramirez, may I take a look at your hip?" Maria exclaimed, "It hurts so bad, the pain is radiating down my entire leg, it feels like sharp needles stabbing me. Can you please help me?" Lydia looks at her and says, "We will take good care of you, Ms. Ramirez." Maria looked at her again and whispered, "Lydia, is that you?" Lydia says, "I will give you something for the pain." Lydia injects an exorbitant amount of pain medication, to keep Maria from talking in front of the nurse. She does not want anyone on staff to know, she personally knows this patient. It would open too many painful wounds from her past. Lydia tells the nurse to order lab work, we need to determine the extent of the infection. Maria is dosing in and out and says, "Why did you leave and not tell us where you went?" Maria falls asleep. The nurse looks at Lydia with a confused look on her face. Lydia explains the pain medication must be working. She is a little delirious. Lydia tells the nurse to order a CT scan and to let her know when all the results are in. Lydia was trying to quickly get as far away from Maria's room as possible.

Lydia goes to the doctors' lounge and just about throws up. She takes in a couple of deep breaths and tries to pull herself together. As she is leaving the doctors' lounge, she sees Maria's father and brother enter her exam room. Lydia breaks out into a sweat and now knows there is no way out of acknowledging them and facing her past. She puts her hands over her face and cries. Then she goes into the bathroom and washes her face. She looks at herself in the mirror and says, "Get it together Lydia and get ready to face your demons!" She hears her name paged on the intercom, Dr. Sanchez. Please come to the nurses' station. She heads that direction and Lydia asks one of the other ER doctors to please take over this patient's care because she has two other critical patients that need her immediate attention.

Lydia gets through the rest of her shift, not running into the Ramirez family. She plans to take a different exit out of the hospital when her shift ends, just in case Maria's brothers know she works there. Lydia worked until eight thirty this morning, which is way past her normal work hours. The stress of seeing the Ramirez family exhausted her. She showers and changes out of her scrubs. As she is leaving, she runs into Dr. Naomi in the hallway. She was on her cell phone whispering and speaking Korean; to someone she called Jamison. Then she changed it and said, Jason. She hears her say to him, "We have a patient at Westgate Memorial, my brother is attending to, that's a match." Lydia slows her walk down to a crawl to see if she can hear more information. She hears Dr. Naomi tell this person to get to the clinic right away. They need a transporter. Dr. Naomi hangs up and calls Myung. While still speaking in Korean, she tells him that Jamison will be there shortly to get the OR room set up. Make sure Jamison's instruments are ready.

Lydia was thinking to herself, *no! this isn't what I think it is. I'm just tired and frustrated, maybe I'm reading too much into that conversation. And besides, there are a lot of men named Jamison, and my Jamison wouldn't understand Korean, anyway.* She brushes it off as she has her own problems to deal with at the moment. She calls Sam, he doesn't answer. She leaves a voice mail message asking, if he wanted to grab lunch.

She goes to the parking garage to leave the hospital. Lydia is shaking, she can barely get into her SUV. She knows Maria was admitted and the Ramirez family is at the hospital with her. So, for now, she is safe. Her cell phone rings. It scares the heck out of her, it's Sam. He says, "Hello beautiful, I'm sorry I missed your call, I was in surgery." Lydia replied, "It is so nice to hear your voice, I really need to see you today, can we meet?" He tells her, he is scheduled do his volunteer work today at the clinic. He reminded her, he told her about his community involvement, when they first met. And how he volunteers two days a week at the clinic in Wicker Park. She says, "Okay, I understand." He tells her, she could come by the clinic later, if she wanted, and he would try to see her in between patients. That some days, they are not terribly busy. Lydia says, "That's okay, I will just go to the gym and then home. It has been a long night so I will see you tomorrow." Sam said, "I will text you the address, just in case you change your mind." Lydia replied, "Okay, I may take you up on that, if I can't sleep."

She heads home, her building is secure, so she knows she is safe for now. Upon arriving in her parking garage, she runs into Kendra. Lydia parks her SUV, and she and Kendra walk to the elevator together. Lydia asked, "You off today?" Kendra replies, "Yes, I took a half day off, to get caught up on some things in my condo." Lydia asked, "What floor do you live on?" Kendra replied, "The top floor, I have a corner unit with a city view and the lake view." Lydia says, "Very nice." Kendra asked if she would like to come up? Lydia replied, "Sure, I would like that." On the elevator ride, Lydia and Kendra make small talk about their career and their hobbies. They have more in common than they thought. Lydia steps into Kendra's condo and is amazed, of how beautiful and spacious it is. This is what Lydia needed, to take her mind off the Ramirez family. Kendra asked Lydia if she would like a drink. Lydia replied, "Yes, please, do you have whiskey? I will take mine neat, please." Kendra's eyes opened wide. She only knows one other person, who orders whiskey this way. Kendra pours herself a glass of wine and says, "To new friendships." Lydia raises her glass and says, "Yes, to a new friendship." It is now eleven o'clock in the morning, and Lydia needs to get some sleep for tonight's shift. She tells Kendra, thanks for the hospitality, but she needed to get some sleep. She then tells her she would invite her down to her place soon.

Lydia gets on the elevator and heads down to her condo. During the elevator ride, she is thinking about all the green cards she sold back in the Bronx. And how she saved a lot of families from being deported. She made enough money to support her family, especially with her sister's medical expenses. And also put herself through college and medical school. She cannot believe her past has found her. She did not understand why the people she was working for started to scammed people. She had gone years of helping undocumented immigrants get real green cards. Then, out of nowhere, people were being arrested and deported because the green cards were fake. She did not know it was a scam until it was too late. Several families were after her because she was the connect. She is the one they gave their money to, and she is the one who brought back the green cards. It was her face they knew and no other. She had to leave the Bronx abruptly and move her parents and sister down to Florida. She moved to Chicago, to be as far away from them as she could, to protect them. She thought they would never find her.

She lay across her bed, as if she were waiting for the authorities to come and arrest her or for the Ramirez family, to come and kill her. She falls asleep! *Maria's brother is standing in the hospital's hallway looking for exam room three. He makes eye contact with Lydia; his face turns red and he balled up both fists. Lydia clinched her chest. He goes into his sister's room. Lydia heads to the parkkng garag to leave the hospital. There is a note on her windshield under the windshield wiper. Lydia takes the note off and read it before getting into her SUV. The note said, we know where you live, and you cannot escape again. You owe me your life and you will pay.*

JAMISON

Things Aren't as They Seem

Jamison has been super busy these last few months. He is doing well in his firm and has four new engineers he is mentoring. His business is also soaring. He has a new patent for another new surgical tool and has sold them to four more major hospitals in other states. The transport business is soaring, to the point he can barely keep up. Jamison just hung up with Dr. Naomi again. She has become increasingly demanding of his time lately. He is having regrets about coming on board with them, but he must stick it out because he knows too much. The money is good, and it is not like he needs it anyway. But it would be extremely dangerous for him, if he tries to leave the organization. This underground market is way deeper than Dr. Naomi, Myung, and Jon.

Jamison's mother left him a half a million dollars from an insurance policy when she died. It was all willed to him because his older brother, Wesley, started using drugs after Jamison went to juvenile jail for eighteen months. Jamison is thinking about the time he spent in juvie jail for a self-defense case. Caleb, the school bully, had been tormenting kids since elementary school. One day during high school, Caleb challenged Jamison to a fight, Caleb was telling everyone, Jamison was soft and a mama's boy. Jamison had ignored him for weeks, but on this particular day, Caleb said Jamison was weak, just like his little sick mama. This sent Jamison into a rage. He hit Caleb only one time, with such force, that Caleb fell and hit his head on the cinder block in the school parking lot. Caleb had brain swelling and died a couple of weeks later from head trauma. Caleb's family could afford to hire the best attorneys, money could buy. They wanted Jamison to pay for their son's death; even though it was an accident and Jamison had never been in a fight or in any kind of trouble. Jamison was an honor roll and a model student; because of the circumstances, the prosecutor was lenient, so they tried Jamison in Juvenile court.

He was sentenced to eighteen months in a juvenile detention center. It was not fair, because Caleb charged at Jamison. Although there were witnesses to confirm this. The court had to make an example out of Jamison for his actions, due it resulting in death. The prosecutor told Jamison's family, if he did not get into any trouble while in Juvenile detention, during the eighteen-month sentence, she would have his records sealed so this offense would not be on his permanent record.

Jamison's mother died during those eighteen months because of kidney failure. He never forgave himself for breaking her heart, by disappointing her and not being present during her last days on earth. When Jamison was sentenced, his older brother Wesley turned to drugs. He felt he should have been there to defend his little brother. He was a senior when this happened and was in basketball practice. He had a promising college scholarship to play basketball. He had career aspirations to become a doctor because of helping to care for his mother. Wesley could not handle the pressure of losing his little brother, and his mother's health was declining. When their mother died, Wesley disappeared after the funeral and no one has seen him since. Jamison buried himself in schoolwork to learn everything he could. He told Lydia, Victoria and Jade that he received academic scholarships to pay for college, but it was his mother's life insurance policy that paid for all of his education. It was easier for him to tell them; it was a scholarship than to explain his hurtful past. He was afraid of being judged, if anyone found out about his time in the juvenile detention center. He feared being labeled as a violent offender, so he kept this part of his life a secret.

Jamison deeply feels guilty for not being there when his mother passed away. He also feels responsible for his brother's drug addiction. He is thinking about this while he is driving to Wicker Park. He has been transporting from all three hospitals to the clinic this past week. It is very time-consuming and tiresome, but he is making it work. His cell phone rings. It is Dr. Naomi. He answers, "Hello." He is thinking to himself, *I just hung up with Dr. Naomi, so why is she calling again?* Dr. Naomi is speaking in Korean, she is telling him to ditch the burner phone and to get another one, same plan as before, to be sure and burn the chip. Jamison looks at the screen on his dashboard and shook his head, then says to Dr. Naomi, in a condescending tone, "Do you think I would forget, it's time to make the switch?" Dr. Naomi replies, "I know we have you very busy and I have to make sure we cover our bases." Jamison replies, "Understood!" And push the button on the screen to end the call. He is rethinking that twenty to thirty grand a week. He says out loud, "Is it really worth it?" He shakes off the frustration as he arrives to the clinic.

He pulls around the back in the medical supply van as normal. He goes inside with his precious cargo and hands it to the nurse, just as he always does. As he walked towards Dr. Naomi's office, he thinks he hears Lydia's voice in Jon's office. It was not unusual for Jon to have female visitors in his office; he lived his life as the lady's man. Jamison was thinking, *no way, there is no way, it would be Lydia, they don't even know each other.* Then he hears Lydia laugh and tell Jon as she was getting closer to the door, "I wouldn't trade it for all the tea in China." Jamison quickly ducks into an empty room to hide. Lydia opens the door, Jon is right behind her, they are holding hands and he gives her a gentle hug and walks her to the front of the clinic. Jamison knows Lydia has been using that phrase since they met twelve years ago. And he recognizes her channel number five cologne. He remained hidden until the hallway was clear. Then he eases towards the back door and gets in the van. He is sitting in the delivery van breathing heavy. He yells out loud, "What the hell Man! That was too close." He is furious, the same as that day back in high school. He promised himself he would never get that angry again.

He waits at least twenty minutes in the van before leaving. He must make sure Lydia is out of the neighborhood, he cannot let her see him. Jamison is thinking about how Lydia has been glowing the past few months, the private conversations where she was whispering and smiling. He puts two and two together and screams, "Jon is Sam?" Jamison put both hands over his face as if he were washing the lies off. Then he remembered the night at the SPOT, when he met Jon there in the champagne room. Jon invited him there, to meet a couple of high-profile surgeons, which was perfect, to introduce his surgical tools. Jamison now remembers leaving Jon and going to their reserved table a little later than normal. Then he remembers leaving Lydia at the bar, with one of her hospital colleagues, she said she would take an Uber home, he didn't need to wait for her. Now Jamison is furious! Jon intentionally set out to meet Lydia that night. What kind of game are they playing? He now knows he has to play it cool and not let either of them know he knows until he figures out why. He heads out and destroys the burner phone at the crematory as planned. He then purchases a new one in the Evanston area. After he picked up the new burner phone, he did his usual and text the team, *thank you* and goes home for the evening.

It's the next morning, and Jamison is at work, sitting at his desk. His phone rings, it's Jade, she is crying hysterically. He can barely understand what she is saying. Finally, he says firmly, "Jade, pull it together, what are you trying to say?" Jade proceeds to tell him that Victoria was in a horrific car accident last night and they are not sure if she will pull through. Jamison couldn't speak, his heart sank. He said, "Jade, what hospital is she in?" Jade said, "Westgate Memorial, I'm heading there now." Jamison said, "I'm on my way." Jade said, "Can you call Lydia, I'm too upset to make the call?" Jamison says, "Sure!" Jamison is thinking, *Lydia is the last person I want to talk to right now, but I have to leave my personal feelings out of it.* He dials her cell phone, and it goes to voice mail. He leaves a message for her to call him right away, it is important that she call him ASAP! Jamison can barely think straight as he rushes over to Westgate Memorial.

JADE

Things Aren't as They Seem

Jade is crying hysterically but pulls herself together to let Mr. Stern know the situation and she must leave for the day. As she is driving to the hospital, she is thinking about her conversation with Nicholas last night. Nicholas had explained to her that grandpa, (her dad) was in renal failure and if he does not receive a kidney soon, he would die. His body can no longer handle dialysis, and it is too much for his heart. Her dad was always a healthy man, he took excellent care of himself and she doesn't understand why he is in renal failure. Nicholas pleads with her to come home to see him. Jade finally agrees to get a red eye flight Friday night and Nicholas would pick her up from the airport and take her straight to the hospital. She made it clear to him she was not going to the house. There are too many awful memories in that house, and Nicholas agreed.

Jade arrives at the hospital; they direct her to the ICU floor where Victoria was. As she approaches the nurses' station, she is taken to a private room to speak to the doctor about Victoria's condition. Jade asked if they could wait because Jamison and Lydia were on the way. She could not bear the news alone. The nurse understood and told her to have a seat. When she was ready, they would page the doctor to come and consult with them. Jade calls Jamison, she tells him she is waiting for him in private room and to hurry. He replied, "I'm five minutes away, and I left Lydia a voice mail message to call me right away, that it is urgent." Jade says to Jamison, "I will call her again, I'm a little calmer know." She then gives Jamison the ICU floor number and tells him she was in a private consultation room waiting for them.

Jade calls Lydia, she answers abruptly as she is panting from the horrible dream she just had. Jade tells her what happened, and that Jamison is on his way. Lydia screams and yells, she is on her way. She will take an Uber to the hospital. Lydia and Jade cry together on the phone. Lydia is scrambling to put on her shoes, grab her coat and keys. She uses the Uber app while still on the phone with Jade and tells her the car will arrive at her building in eight to ten minutes. Neither of them wants to hang up. Jade notices the change in Lydia's tone and says, "Lydia, are you still there?" Lydia is thinking, *I feel like this is another frightful dream,* as she walks to the elevator. Jade knew they were still connected because she could hear Lydia breathing heavily. Finally, Lydia replied, "Yes dear, I'm here. I may lose you as I am getting on the elevator." Lydia's heart sank. She leans her body against the elevator wall and practically slides down, onto the floor. She is thinking about her suspicion with Sam suddenly. Now the Ramirez family is after her, and Victoria is in ICU. She put her hands on the top of her head and yells, "What next! This has to be the worst day of my life."

She is in the Uber and she listens to her voice mail messages. It's Jamison, telling her to call him right away, it's urgent. Lydia cries out, the driver asked, "Maim, are you okay?" She pulls herself together and tells him, "Yes, I'm fine, just please hurry and get me to Westgate Memorial Hospital."

Jamison has arrived, he and Jade are speaking with the doctor about Victoria's condition. They decided not to wait for Lydia. The doctor tells them, she has head trauma and brain swelling, but her vital signs are stable. She was unconscious last night when the EMS brought her in. The CT scan shows severe trauma to the left side of her body. We performed emergency surgery last night to stop the internal bleeding. The critical concern now is the brain swelling. Jade starts to cry, and Jamison sheds a slight tear of his own. He was trying to remain strong for Jade, but he could not help that tiny tear that shed down his cheek. Jamison asked, "Can we see her now?" The doctor replied, "Yes, but I want to warn you. Her head and face are extremely swollen. We put her in a medically induced coma so her brain can rest. She cannot respond to you, okay!" They both shake their heads in unison, to let the doctor know they understand. The doctor escorts them to her room. Upon entry, Jade breaks down and cries. Jamison also sheds several tears. He walks over to Victoria's bed and holds her swollen hand. The doctor explained again about the swelling and if the medication did not work, they would have to drill a small hole in her head to release the fluid. Jade let out a louder cry, Jamison catches her just before she hit the floor. The nurse pulled up a chair close to Victoria's bed. Jamison helps Jade to the chair as she collapsed into the seat. He stands there in silence, listening to the monitors beep and the sound of a ventilator as it pushes air in and out of Victoria's body. With each breath, they watch her chest raise up and down. They are in total silence, even the crying has ceased.

Lydia sends Jade a text, she has arrived and is on her way to ICU. Jade tells Jamison, she would meet Lydia at the elevators, to prepare her for what she is about to see. Jamison look at her with a stern look of disbelief and says, "Lydia looks at this every day. She is a doctor and a surgeon, you know." Jade just gets up and leave the room. Jamison is just standing at Victoria's bedside, staring at all the tubes, and he's thinking about his mother. He is now wondering if this is how she took her last breath. Did she have tubes and monitors? He never had a chance to tell her goodbye.

The nurse comes in and startles Jamison as he was in deep thought. She needed him to step out of the room for a few minutes as they prepare for shift change. As he is leaving the room, he runs into Jade and Lydia. Jamison tells them they are doing a shift change. They needed to wait in the waiting room for about thirty minutes. Lydia is asking, how did this happen? She is crying, she looks at Jamison and says to him. "What are we going to do?" Jamison was explaining what the doctor said and Lydia stops him and says, "I called one of my colleagues that works here, she filled me in on Victoria's condition." Jade says, "Is it as bad as it looks?" Lydia says, "I'm afraid it is, the next twenty-four hours will be critical." Jade says, "You mean she could die?" Lydia nods her head. They hug each other.

CHAPTER TEN

What Have I Done

BRIDGET AND CALVIN

What Have I Done?

Bridget arrives at the bank and discovers Victoria has not arrived yet. This is unusual for her because she is always there at least an hour before the staff arrives. An hour goes by, one of the bank tellers asked Bridget if Victoria was coming in today. Bridget checks her cell phone, to make sure she hadn't missed a call from her. Bridget dials Victoria's cell phone, no answer. She tells the teller that Victoria must have had a doctor's appointment and she was certain she would be in later this morning. She only said that to ease the worrid look on the teller's face. She then calls Victoria's home phone, no answer.

Just as she was about to call her cell again, her cell phone rang. The caller ID shows Chuck. This was the code name for Calvin. She found it strange for him to call her this early, and besides, he knows she is at work. She answers, "Hello, this better be important, to call my cell during business hours." Calvin is silent, he can barely speak. He rumbled some words that Bridget could not understand. Bridget says, "Calvin, what is it? You are not making any sense. I can't understand anything you are saying." Calvin finally says, "Have you seen the news?" Bridget says, "No, I barely watch the news, with all the crime in Chicago, I don't waste my morning listening to all of that negativity. But why do you ask?" Calvin slowly says, "It's Victoria. She was in a terrible car accident last night. She is in critical condition, the news said, the vehicle was totaled." They are both silent and in disbelief, Bridget sheds a tear. Calvin says, "It happened near the casino. The news said something about her going at a high rate of speed, and she blew through an intersection and was T-boned by a semi-truck." Calvin says sadly, "She may not make it." Bridget asked, "What hospital is she in?" Calvin replied, "I had to call around and tell them I was her brother to find out. She is at Westgate Memorial in ICU." Bridget gasp for air and said to Calvin, "I have to go now, I need to call the hospital. I will call you back." Bridget cries. She is very fond of Victoria and looks up to her as a mentor. Bridget calls Westgate Memorial explains her relationship with Victoria. They could not release any information about her condition. Bridget is now frantic and tries to pull herself together. She explains to the assistant manager she has a family emergency and has to go home.

Calvin's mind is racing, he is deeply concerned about Victoria. He still loved her as much today, as he did when he first laid eyes on her, in the fourth grade. He was thinking about how mangled her SUV was and how no one could have survived that impact. He is thinking about last night's events. He remembered she left the casino early. The news comes on again and now he is more attentive to the details of the accident. He locks in on the time and location of the accident. He grabs his chest and realized the accident occurred right after she left the casino. From the location of the accident, Victoria was en route home.

His phone rings, it's Bridget, she says, "I have to leave work, I cannot function, I feel like I will have a breakdown again." Calvin asked, "Did you find out anything about her condition?" Bridget says, "No, the hospital would not give me any information." She then asked Calvin, "Did you find out any more information?" Calvin shares the recent information he has with her, she exclaims, "Oh no! Do you think she saw us last night?" Calvin says, "Wow, I didn't think of that. This could explain why she was driving at such a high rate of speed." Bridget says, "I cannot handle this, what did we do?" Calvin says, "Calm down and pull yourself together, Bridget. We have been extremely careful, so I know she did not see us. Maybe she was driving so fast because of the amount of money she lost?" Bridget says, "I sure hope so because I cannot handle it, if we are responsible for her accident." Bridget tells Calvin she is heading home to lie down and take something for her headache and anxiety. She said she will try to reach Jade, to get more information on Victoria's condition.

During the drive home, Bridget is lost in thought, with pain and sorrow for allowing Calvin to her involve in his revenge against Victoria. But he seems genuinely concerned about her condition. She could hear the hurt and pain in his voice. She is thinking about her own car accident from about seven months ago. How traumatizing it was for her. Victoria's accident is far worse.

Bridget's cell phone rings. It is Stewart, the assistant bank manager. He called to inform her, Jade called to let the bank know about Victoria's horrific accident, and it did not look good according to the doctors. She has severe head trauma, with brain swelling, she has a broken femur, ankle, shoulder and a broken left hip. He continued to tell Bridget. They put her in a medically induced coma and if her brain continued to swell, they would have to drill a hole in her head to release the fluid and pressure. Stewart told her to rest up over the weekend, because starting Monday they would have to fill Victoria's shoes for a while. He will need her to get him up to speed on all her projects. Bridget had to pull over as she could not drive at this point. She was hysterical and devastated by the news.

Bridget enters her apartment, she goes to the kitchen, pours herself a huge glass of water and takes three Percocet. Her head was throbbing so badly, she could barely walk. As she lies on her sofa and turns on the television, the news comes on. She catches a glimpse of the wreckage. She now sees for herself, what Calvin had told her about the accident and how bad it was. Now she understands why he said he doesn't know how anyone could have survived the accident. Bridget could not tell the vehicle was an SUV, because it was so twisted and mangled. Just before she falls asleep, she calls Jade, no answer. Bridget left a voice mail message stating how sorry she was to hear about Victoria and to please keep her informed, as the hospital would not give her any information.

Calvin goes to Westgate Memorial. He could not bear, not knowing her condition for himself. Deep down inside, he felt responsible because he has been stalking her for almost a year. At the time, he had no idea of what would happen when he was actually faced to face with her. But he definitely did not plan for anything to happen to her. He yells out while driving to the hospital, *"Oh God! What have I done?"*

VICTORIA, LYDIA, JAMSON, JADE

What Have I Done?

They are still at the hospital, waiting for Victoria to open her eyes. The doctor comes in and asks, who is Victoria's next of kin? They each look at each other and Jamison says, "Her parents, but they live in San Mateo, California." Jade asked, "Why do you need to know that. Are you saying she will not make it?" The doctor says, "It's just a formality, we need to get paperwork signed for consent so we will have it, if we need it." He exits Victoria's room. They are finally alone, no nurses or doctors in the room. They discuss with each other how to get in touch with her parents. Lydia says, "We have been together for twelve years and I have no idea what her parents' names are." Jade says, "I know her mom is a big real estate broker in San Mateo." Jamison says, "Oh, and her father has his own investment firm. It shouldn't be hard to find them. Google realestate broker last name Ellis in San Mateo, California, and see what comes up. I will search for an investment firm, last name Ellis." Jade says, "For her not to tell us about her parents, maybe we should wait and see if she wakes up." Jamison exclaims, "We have to call them to let them know, we do not have the right to keep this from them. No matter the personal relationship. They are her parents and they deserve to know how critical her condition is." Jade replies, "You're right, I understand."

While they are doing their research, Jade checks her voice mail messages. The first one is from Bridget at the bank. The second one is from her nephew Nicholas. He was very chipper and said, I can't wait to see you tonight, aunt Jade. I know grandma and grandpa will be glad to see you. Call me as soon as you get on the airplane tonight. Jade puts her hand on her head because she totally forgot about this trip after learning of Victoria's accident. Jade is thinking to herself; *I will need to cancel my flight for tonight. I can't leave Victoria.* Lydia sees the look on Jade's face and asked, "Is everything okay?" Jade says, "Yes, I was planning to take a red eye flight tonight, to go see my father back home. He is in the hospital in renal failure. I planned to leave after the SPOT tonight." They each looked at Victoria when Jade said the SPOT. They were silent for a few minutes, then Jamison says, "Jade, why didn't you tell us? We would not have let you go through this by yourself." Lydia says, "Yeah Jade, we are family and we support each other." Jade says, "I apologize but you all have so much going on and I didn't want to worry you. I was returning home on Sunday morning, so it was just going to be for one day." Jamison retorts, "No more secrets, we are family and we support each other through the good times and the bad times." They each agree.

Lydia encourages Jade to take the flight, she would keep her updated on Victoria's condition. She says to Jade, "Victoria will be in this medically induced coma for at least a few more days, unless the swelling gets worse. We will just be sitting here, so go see your father." Jamison says, "I agree with Lydia, I don't want you to regret not seeing him if something happens. Besides, Victoria would want you to be with your family." Jade sheds a tear and says, "You said that as if she is already gone." Jamison replied, "You know that's not how I meant it. Even if it were not for the accident and we had our usual Friday night get together, we would encourage you to be with your family."

Jamison is becoming irritated with Jade overreacting to every word he says. He is just as upset as they are; maybe even more, since his recent discovery of Lydia and Sam, Jon or whatever his name is. Jamison receives a call on his cell phone. Since he did not recognize the number, he told the ladies; he would take this call out in the hallway. Jamison answers, "Hello, this is Jamison." It was a male on the other end. He said, "This is Preston Ellis, I received a voice mail message from you and that it was urgent that I returned your call." Jamison says, "Yes sir, I'm best friends with your daughter Victoria and she has been in a horrible car accident." The phone went silent, Jamison says, "Hello, Mr. Ellis, are you still there?" Mr. Ellis cleared his throat and said, "Yes son, I'm still here, how bad is it?" Jamison explained the details of what he knew, gave them the name of the hospital and her ICU room number. He informed them of the need for them to sign consent papers in the event they have to drill a hole in her head if the swelling didn't stop. Mr. Ellis said, "Whatever is needed, son, her mother and I will provide it. Can you give the hospital this fax number to send the forms and we will sign them and send them back right away." Jamison says, "Yes sir, I will make sure of it." Jamison walks over to the charge nurse and gives her the information to fax the consent forms to Victoria's parents.

Jamison's emotions are all over the place. This is the first time he has been alone since he arrived at the hospital. He has not sorted out his feelings for what he witnessed at the clinic and now Victoria. His cell phone rings again, this time it's his firm asking if he was coming back to the office today. Jamison says, "Oh my goodness, I forgot to call you. Can you please transfer me to Mr. Kushner? I have a personal emergency and please let everyone know, I will not be back in the office today." Jamison speaks with Mr. Kushner directly and explains what has happened. His boss tells him to take as much time as he needs and to keep them posted.

Dr. Naomi calls the burner phone. She tells Jamison she has another transport for him. He tells her he has an emergency; he was at Westgate Memorial, so he could not transport today. He is not leaving Victoria's side. Dr. Naomi says in a stern voice, "Yes, I'm aware of Victoria's condition and I assure you as a surgeon myself, she will be fine for now. The equipment we need is actually at Westgate Memorial, and all you have to do is bring it to the clinic. It's just an hour away. You will be back in about two hours." Jamison was pretty ticked off and was going to tell Dr. Naomi what she could do with her equipment, but he suddenly remembered what he had seen yesterday at the clinic and his anger intensified. He says to Dr. Naomi, "Okay! where do I make the pickup?" Jamison goes back into Victoria's room to let Lydia and Jade know the call was from Victoria's father. The hospital is faxing consent forms to Mr. Ellis's office now. Both parents will sign right away. Jade says, "Oh good!" Lydia has a look of relief on her face. Jamison then tells them he must leave for a couple of hours. He forgot about a client he was meeting with this afternoon. He will be quick and to please forgive him for having to leave. Lydia says, "You are good, take care of your business, we will let you know if her condition changes." Jade shakes her head in agreement. Jamison goes over to Victoria, holds her swollen hand and says, "I will be right back V, keep your eyes peeled." He left the room.

Lydia's mind is racing everywhere. Not to mention, she did not have much sleep because of being awakened from an awful dream to a nightmare. She is trying to rationalize with the events that have taken place over the last twenty-four hours. She is in deep thought and she doses off to sleep. Jade looks over at Lydia, she gets a blanket to cover her up and a pillow for her head. Jade steps out of the room to make a phone call.

Lydia falls into a deep sleep. She dreams the same dream she had earlier this morning. This time, the Ramirez brothers have brought the old neighborhood to the hospital. They are all standing in the lobby like mobsters, demanding to see her. Lydia leaves the hospital early and sneaks out through the security entrance. She calls an Uber to take her home because she didn't want to take a chance going to the parking garage. As she is standing there waiting for her ride, someone yells, there she is, let's get her. Lydia is now running down the street, screaming and trying to get away from them. She trips and falls to the ground. They catch up with her. They are yelling and screaming at her and just as they were hitting and kicking her, Jade is standing over her saying, "Lydia, wake up, you are having a bad dream." Lydia opens her eyes and says, *"Oh God! What have I done?"* Jade is confused by her statement and says to her, "I'm here, you were having a bad dream, you were yelling stop, I didn't do it and you were panting extremely hard. It must have been a terrible dream, but It's okay, you are safe."

Jamison is now in route to the clinic. He is praying Jon has already left because he does not want to see him or hear his lying mouth. He now wishes more than ever, he had told Dr. Naomi to find someone else. He calls Jade to find out if Victoria's condition had changed, Jade tells him, there are no changes in her condition. She says to him, "Be careful and take your time. Everything is the same here. I can't handle anything happening to you." Jamison says, "Don't worry, I promise to make it back in one piece." She could hear a smile in his voice. She then says, "Jamison!" He answers, "Yes", she says, "I'm sorry for being short with you earlier, I really didn't mean to be snappy." Jamison says, "No worries dear, we are good, and we are all in this together. Keep your eyes peeled." Jade smiled; they hang up.

Jamison is thinking about how it is time for him to leave the underground business. After Victoria's accident and now Jade's father, he is thinking about how precious life is. He needs to go see his father and find his brother. He says out loud, "It's time!" He arrives at the clinic, enters the back door with his key. As he is walking down the hallway with the package, he hears Dr. Myung and Dr. Naomi in her office. He avoids them both and takes the package to the receptionist. As he's leaving, Dr. Myung calls him to join them in his office, it's payday. Jamison had totally forgotten because of the accident.T hese people cover their tracks very well, they handle all transactions in cash. As Jamison was picking up his envelope, he notices the amount written on it. Fifty thousand dollars. Jamison says, "This is more than my usual cut, I know I have made a few extra pickup's this week, but fifty thousand dollars for one week?" Dr. Naomi says, "We had some high paying clients this week. You were carrying premium packages, that is your cut."

Jamison says, "Well, I will have to leave the business, I'm overloaded at my firm. The late nights and unexpected runs are interfering with my career. The money is great but it's not about the money, it's about my time." Just as he finishes, Jon walks in the office to get his pay for the week. Jamison's head is steaming hot, he tries to keep his cool. Dr. Naomi says, "What are you trying to say Jamison?" Jamison replied, "I'm saying, this is it for me! I'm done as of today." He then looks over at Jon with fire in his eyes.

Dr. Naomi says, "It doesn't work like that Jamison, there is no quitting in the underground organization, you are a smart man, you should know this." Jamison says, "Well, I'm done, and that's final." Jon says, "Do you think you joined the business without collateral?" Dr. Naomi then says, "Do you think Victoria's accident was an accident?" Jamison has that feeling boiling inside, as he did back in high school. He looks at Jon and says, "So, is that why you went after Lydia and told her your name was Sam?" Jon replies, "Let's just say she is a security deposit." Jamison is so upset; he abruptly leaves the office and slams the door. He gets in the van to take it to the parking spot. He was silent the entire ride. For the second time in his life, he was not in control. He parked the van in the usual spot. He never had Uber pick him up there and he never parked his personal vehicle there either. This time, he walked five blocks to let off some steam before calling for an Uber. Once he stopped walking, he stood still. He looked up at the sky and yelled, *"Oh God! What have I done?"*

Jade left the hospital to go home, to get comfortable clothes for the hospital stay tonight. Her thoughts are all over the place. Nicholas called her again to confirm the time to pick her up at the airport and to tell her how excited he is to finally see her. Jade explains the turn of events that has taken place and says to him, "I really don't want to leave my best friend, who is lying in ICU fighting for her life." She explained how she can come next week instead. Nicholas said to her in a sad voice, "The doctors said earlier today, he will be lucky to make it through the next twenty-four hours." Jade could hear the sadness in his voice and said, "I will be there, pick me up at three thirty in the morning, and remember, I'm not going anywhere except for the hospital." Nicholas was so excited and yet sad at the same time. They hang up.

Jade is home now and has a small carry-on suitcase packed. She takes an Uber to the airport, but before leaving home; she called Lydia to check on Victoria. Lydia assures her Victoria's condition has not changed, which is a good thing. This means her brain has ceased swelling. She tells Jade to get on that plane and to go see her father, Jamison is in the background, confirming that she goes.

Jade says, "Okay, I'm heading to the airport now." Jamison takes Lydia's phone and tells Jade; he loves her and to be careful. He demanded she calls him as soon as she arrives, no matter what time it is. Jade says, "I will, and I love you and Lydia as well; put the phone next to Victoria's head and put me on speaker, please." She whispers softly, with a trembling voice, "Victoria, we love you and I will see you tomorrow night." Lydia and Jamison look at each other with sadness and they both say in unison, "We love you Victoria and we love you Jade." Jamison looks over at Lydia, and he is feeling guilty about being short and angry with her, for not telling him about Sam. He says, "I'm sorry if I was short with you today." They hugged each other tightly in silence as they listen to the monitors beep and the sound of the ventilator.

Jade's flight lands, she is coming down the tarmac and she sees what looks like Nicholas standing there waiting for her. As she gets closer, she realizes it is Nicholas. She is wondering, how in the heck was he standing in a secured area of the airport? She says, "Nicholas?" He exclaims, "It's so nice to see you auntie!" He gives her an enormous bear hug. She can't believe how big he is in person. She asked him. "How in the world did you get access to the tarmac?" He tells her he works at the airport part time, so he has security clearance. She smiles as he took her small carry on and realizes this is the first time, she has smiled all day.

They get in his SUV, she tells him, "I see you have a wonderful taste in vehicles, just as I." They have small talk during the ride to the hospital. Nicholas asked her what time her return flight is tomorrow. She reminds him the return flight is for today. Saturday! They arrive at the hospital and head to the ICU wing. Upon arriving, she sees her mother and both sisters in the waiting area. They all run up to hug her and to tell her, her father just passed away. Her name was the last thing he said, before he took his last breath. Jade screams as she falls to the floor, *"Oh God, what have I done!"*

DR. NAOMI LEE

She and her brother Jon were born and raised in Yeouido, Seoul Korea. Naomi's birth name is Min-Jee Koh, which means brightness and wisdom. Her brother Jon's birth name is Man-Shik Koh, which means deeply rooted.

Yeouido is a large island in central Seoul, that is easily accessible by metro and taxi. Yeouido-dong is the major finance district of Seoul. It's the home of one of South Korea's biggest broadcasting companies, KBS. It is also home to the National Assembly, the seat of South Korea's government. It is Seoul's main finance and investment banking districts, including the Korea Exchange Center. The main attraction in Yeouido-dong is Yeouido Park. This space was once a big, empty village square, built on a former runway. It is now filled with green spaces, waterways and native trees. The park has a real forest feel to it.

Their father owns the Conrad Seoul, it is a luxury five-star hotel located in Seoul's main finance and investment banking district. The lobby has a spiral staircase that is one hundred and nineteen feet and nine inches, connecting the lobby to the tenth floor. This hotel has four hundred and forty guest rooms, and the penthouse is just a little over three thousand square feet. Other amenities include ballrooms, meeting rooms, a bar and restaurant, and a twenty-four-hour fitness center. It overlooks the beautiful Han River, and it is recognized as one of the top hotels in Korea.

Naomi and her brother Jon are the only children. They grew up very wealthy. It's the success of the Hotel that paid for them to go to college and medical school in the United States. Her parents were not happy with either of them because they wanted them both to stay and take over the hotel business. Naomi is the firstborn. Which was a disappointment for her dad, because he did not want a girl at all. He made sure she knew how he felt as she watched him favor Jon throughout their childhood and adult life. He would often tell Naomi how disappointed he was that she was born. Her mother did not stand up to her father, but she would secretly give Naomi love and attention. The big city life and luxury living was not unusual for the Koh's, which is where Naomi gets her snobby demeanor and her harsh tone.

She moved to Chicago from Boston with her husband after

completing medical school at Harvard University and eight years of residency at Massachusetts General hospital (Mass General). She met her husband Myung Lee while she was a resident. He is quite a few years older than she, and he was a well-established top heart surgeon on staff at Mass General. They dated for the first four years of her residency and married during the last four.

She lives in the Wicker Park neighborhood. She chose this neighborhood because of the urban feel, and it's rated as one of the best places to live in Chicago. She opened a free clinic in her neighborhood that she, her brother and husband run. They each volunteer there to service their communities. The staff are all family members of her husband, Myung. This is how they can operate their underground business.

Naomi developed her short, harsh attitude from her childhood. Not to mention, being wealthy as a child, she learned very early about **us** and **them**. The rich and the poor, no in-between. Her family looked down on the poor people. Their parents told them it was their fault for being poor. They could only socialize with the elite upper-class people. She carried this attitude with her through college and med school. She has always been competitive, thanks to her father, because she always had to go above and beyond to please him. He wouldn't accept anything less than perfection from her.

Naomi studied very hard throughout her life, so she never developed people skills. She did, however, become the best academically. Her goal was to become the top surgeon in the world, and that she did. Myung does not carry those same beliefs and thoughts about people, but because he loves Naomi so much, he tolerates her snobbish behavior. Just as her mother tolerated her dad's behavior, by turning the other way. Myung is also the top cardiologist in the country. Together, they are remarkably successful and wealthy. She got into the underground business because of greed. She saw an opportunity to gain more wealth, because she feared becoming one of those poor people. She never gave back to her community or anyone else. She doesn't like Jamison; she saw an opportunity to have her needs met. She loves control and power. Transplanting organs for the rich and wealthy give her a thrill. She feels that the poor don't need them, so why not keep the rich alive, instead of making them wait for years on the donor list? After all, it is their fault they are poor.

Her clinic is a cover-up for their underground business. Myung just went along with whatever she wants to avoid confrontation, but he also like the money this business has to offer. They make more money in the underground business in one weekend than they make in a week, as top surgeons.

The Story Continues

The Chronicles Of
Integrated Friends *Jamison's Story*

Coming

6.21.21

Jamison's Story

It's Saturday morning, it's been a long week and several endless nights at the hospital with Victoria. Jamison is out of his normal routine because of work, Victoria and Dr. Naomi. This lifestyle is taking a toll on his mind and body. He heads to the gym to clear his head and burn off some stress. "Hey Mr. Jamison," the young man says, "I haven't seen you in a while, how have you been?" Jamison lifts his head off the bench press, sweaty with an irritated look on his face. He says, "Hey Youngblood, how's it going?" The eager young man replies, "It's going great man, I've been working out every day, can you see my rip?" Jamison looks at him with a smile and says, "Yeah, I see it, great job!" He put his headphones up to his ear and starts to bench press again. The young man knows this is a sign, and it's time for him to go. Jamison is thinking over his life, his career, his brother, his parents and his alternate lifestyle. He feels so guilty for Victoria being in the hospital in a coma and Jade jeopardizing her chance of becoming a partner by representing Dr. Naomi. He is furious. He got his best friends wrapped up in his mess, oh how he wishes, he could take it all back, and resume life as it was, prior to saying yes to Dr. Naomi.

He finishes his work out and goes to the men's dressing room, to shower and get ready for the day. As soon as he enters, his cell phone rings. It's Dr. Naomi, Jamison answered, "Why are you calling my regular phone?" Dr. Naomi replies, "You did not answer or return my calls when I called the business phone." Jamison suddenly realizes he forgot it at home and explained to Dr. Naomi, he accidentally left it at home. "What's up Doc?" She answers, "We need a transporter, call me on the business phone as soon as you get home." Jamison agrees and head to the shower. While in the shower, he is disgusted with the recent choices he has made. He says out loud, as the water is flowing down his head and face. "I have to get out of this by any means necessary, and I mean any means necessary."

He is home, checks the business phone, and sure enough he has four miss calls from Dr. Naomi and two from Jon. Now Dr. Naomi, he can tolerate but Jon, Sam or whatever his name is, makes the blood rush to his head. He calls Dr. Naomi back. She gives him details on the pickup location and time. He hangs up without saying, keep your eyes peeled. Jamison wants to connect with Kendra tonight. It has been a couple of weeks because of the unexpected events happening in his life right now. Kendra had already told him to take care of his business and not to worry, she wasn't going anywhere. After all, she moved to the city to be closer to him. So, he thinks!

Acknowledgements

First, I want to thank God most of all, because without God I wouldn't be able to do any of this. Having an idea and turning it into a book is as hard as it sounds. The experience is both internally challenging and rewarding.

Although this period of my life was filled with many ups and downs, I'm thankful to each one of my family and friends for encouraging me and believing in my dream. Especially, for putting up with me throughout the arduous process of writing this novel.

I owe an enormous debt of gratitude to those who gave me detailed and constructive comments. Special thanks to Chuck E. Williams for being the first person to read this novel in its most raw and unedited format.

I especially want to thank my daughter Symone Weemes for providing emotional support to start this journey and for holding me accountable when I wanted to give up.

Additionally, I want to give special acknowledgements to everyone below for providing their services to help make my dream a reality:

Book Cover Design: SymoneRae Designs
Photographer: Stills N Motion
Lashes: Dae Jackson, Pretty Handsome Beauty & Barber Studios
Makeup: Ashlynn Peggins

Author's Bio

Rose has an MBA from Indiana Wesleyan University and a bachelor's degree from Indiana Institute of Technology in Business Administration with Human Resources concentration.

She has worked in corporate America in the Transportation Industry for the past thirty-five years; twenty-two of those years were with the same company, working in various roles.

She won many young author awards as a young child and has always wanted to be a published writer. Now that her children are adults and living their lives, she decided to pursue her dream as a writer in 2018.

Rose is a member of the National Writers Association and Authors Alliance. Her first book is a novel, The Chronicles of "Integrated Friends"

Stay tuned for the second book of the sequel: The Chronicles of Integrated Friends: Jamison's Story.
coming June, 21-2021

Author Rosej

www.ingramcontent.com/pod-product-compliance
Lightning Source LLC
Chambersburg PA
CBHW050244110726
4789BCB00007B/2265